"*I won't go to bed with you, Mr. Cade.*"

Zoe felt herself drown in confusion as a vivid mental picture of the two of them together, naked limbs entwined, presented itself with shocking clarity.

"I wasn't asking you to," James mocked. Zoe felt herself cringe at the pointed put-down. "But if the time ever came when I *did* want to go to bed with you, I would. Make no mistake about that, Miss Kilgerran!"

DIANA HAMILTON is a true romantic at heart and fell in love with her husband at first sight. They still live in the fairy-tale Tudor house where they raised their three children. Now the idyll is shared with eight rescued cats and a puppy. But despite an often chaotic life-style, ever since she learned to read and write Diana has had her nose in a book— either reading or writing one—and plans to go on doing just that for a very long time to come.

Books by Diana Hamilton

HARLEQUIN PRESENTS
1588—SAVAGE OBSESSION
1641—THREAT FROM THE PAST
1690—LEGACY OF SHAME
1732—SEPARATE ROOMS
1716—THE LAST ILLUSION
1775—NEVER A BRIDE

Don't miss any of our special offers. Write to us at the following address for information on our newest releases.

Harlequin Reader Service
U.S.: 3010 Walden Ave., P.O. Box 1325, Buffalo, NY 14269
Canadian: P.O. Box 609, Fort Erie, Ont. L2A 5X3

DIANA HAMILTON

Sweet Sinner

Harlequin Books

TORONTO • NEW YORK • LONDON
AMSTERDAM • PARIS • SYDNEY • HAMBURG
STOCKHOLM • ATHENS • TOKYO • MILAN
MADRID • WARSAW • BUDAPEST • AUCKLAND

ISBN 0-373-11841-4

SWEET SINNER

First North American Publication 1996.

CHAPTER ONE

'TAKE your hands *off* me!' Zoe twisted her legs away from the driver and endeavoured to cover the expanse of her fishnet-covered thighs with the skirt of the coat she wore flung casually over her shoulders just as the souped-up Mini took a corner on two wheels, the dipped headlights revealing yet another narrow London back street, a figure, gender unguessable-at, leaning against a darkened, vandalised lamp-post.

'Off, I said!' Small though she was, Zoe could shout when she had to. She pushed at the groping hand. She couldn't remember his name, but he had to be drunk, or mad. She ground her teeth with rage as she heard him say thickly, 'Quit foolin' around. You're after a bit of fun and I'm equipped to provide it. What the hell else do you think we're doing here?'

She was not going to answer that. And yelled instead, 'Stop the car!' And much to her surprise, and deep relief, he did, brakes screeching, rubber burning on to tarmac.

Scrabbling to unfasten her seat-belt, reaching for the door release, her fingers all panic-stricken thumbs, she felt herself helped out with a violent shove of his hands, heaving her on to the pavement—which was now miraculously fully illuminated—her handbag following and landing on top of her inelegantly sprawling form, his voice slating as he shouted, 'Little cheat!' before shooting away with a roar of protesting horsepower.

Her breath sobbing between her teeth, Zoe got shakily to her feet, pushed the wildly curling mane of bright blonde hair out of her eyes and bent to retrieve the scattered contents of her handbag. Her coat fell away from her shoulders, pooling on the ground as she hauled herself upright again, only now recognising the source of that sudden illumination. The long, slinky lines of a stationary vehicle were just discernible behind the glare of headlights.

For a moment she was too petrified to move, her heart thumping as if it would beat its way right out of her chest. And her knees were grazed where they'd taken the brunt of her ignominious landing. She couldn't have run if someone had paid her.

Out of the frying pan... All alone and no one in sight... Even the lamp-post-leaner had disappeared. No taxis cruising this area. No one came to these mean streets in one of the least salubrious parts of London unless they lived here or were driving through, taking a short cut.

Someone exited the car. She heard the expensive clunk of metal and saw the impressive height, the intimidating breadth of the man as his shadowed form moved forward into the beam of the lights.

Green eyes widened between thickly mascaraed lashes and stayed that way as she fought to compress the trembling of her lush scarlet mouth. For the first time in her twenty-five years she was frightened witless. Back in the car, with that nameless creep, she had been angry and outraged. But this was different. And she was too terrified to take her eyes from the menace of his measured approach to retrieve her coat to cover herself...

One small hand tugged ineffectively at the narrow tube of tacky black satin that barely covered the crotch of her fishnet tights while the other flew to cover the cleavage afforded by her black, sequinned top. Heavy gilt bracelets jangled and she swayed on her spindly scarlet heels and desperately wished she had secreted a hat-pin about her scantily clad person.

'Were you hurt?' The dark, gravelly voice was abrasive and she took a small, defensive backward step, shaking her head, just wanting him to go away, shivering uncontrollably now despite the heavy warmth of the June night air. 'There have to be better ways of earning a crust.' The wide slash of his mouth indented cynically. 'Don't you understand the risks you're running?'

Mutely staring at him, Zoe tried to find a tart streetwise comment to throw in his face. She failed, her quick wits deserting her, hysteria threatening as immediate fear receded just a little.

She would never forget his face. Never. Thrown into harsh relief by the lights, his features were too austere to be handsome in the popular sense. Arrogant self-assurance rode on slanting cheekbones, on the long straight line of his nose, the determined sweep of his jaw, while the incisive moulding of his mouth was an essay in cruel sensuality and the gleam of his eyes was pure, unadulterated cynicism.

Wide shoulders swooped as he bent to pick up her coat, flinging it at her, dark hair gleaming in the lights.

'Cover yourself. If you've got a shred of sense you'll get back home, out of harm's way. How old are you, anyway? Fifteen?' He didn't wait for an answer; his sort never did, she thought as she clutched the edges of her coat tightly together and heard him ask, 'Where do you live?'

'Peckham Rye,' she managed squeakily, because this time it seemed he did expect an answer and if he thought she would accept his offer to take her there then he would have to think again. She'd rather take her chances and walk. She had never felt so demeaned in the whole of her life.

The offer, however, failed to materialise. He told her instead, 'I'll get you a taxi. I take it you've earned enough to cover the fare.'

He strode away and, her cheeks burning beneath her heavy make-up, she teetered after him, her mental faculties regrouping at long last. She was going to tell him a thing or two! What gave him the all-fired right to sit in judgement?

But he was feeding terse directions into the handset of his car phone and when he had finished she spluttered out, 'The way I earn my living is nothing to do with you! And anyway, you've got everything wrong. I'm——'

'Save the justifications. I don't want to know. A taxi should be here in a matter of minutes. I'll wait until it gets here.' He left the car again, towering above her, his features a mask of bored indifference now as he told her, 'Next time you let yourself get into the kind of trouble you were in tonight just remember that the odds against someone happening by to pick up the pieces are extremely long. A million to one, at a guess.'

He looked as if he deeply regretted the impulse to stop and investigate, to make sure that the tarty object he'd witnessed being hurled out of a barely stationary car hadn't sustained any incapacitating injuries.

Zoe turned huffily away, uncomfortably aware that the few words he'd allowed her to get out must have reinforced his definition of her morals. Non-existent. She was not going to thank him for finding her a taxi. Why should she? The opening to lecture and moralise, jump up on his high horse, was all the recompense he could look for. She was far too sore in mind and body to look at the situation from his point of view.

Too drained by events to argue further, she waited in defeated silence until the black cab arrived, gave the driver her home address and climbed into the back with her nose at a haughty angle, not looking at her pious knight-errant because she knew she would die of embarrassment if she did. And sat in the back devising a hundred and one ways of doing Gary Fletcher to death.

'When I agreed to rent part of your house I didn't know I'd be sharing with a low-down, rotten, treacherous fink!' Zoe limped into the kitchen, her mane of blonde hair still wet from the shower and thankfully free of last night's riotous curls.

'And good morning to you, too.' Gary was deep in the morning edition of the tabloid he worked on and his bluntly good looking features wore a beatific expression as he hitched it down and smiled at her over the top. 'Breakfast?'

'An abject apology would be preferable,' Zoe grumbled. She hadn't slept, she'd been too embarrassed by recent events, and just to pile on the agony she was sore all over this morning. 'But if that's too much to expect from a hard-nosed reporter I'll settle for coffee. Fresh, black and strong.' She swivelled back towards the door. 'In ten minutes.' Adding darkly, 'I'm due at the office by ten, but I'll speak to you later!'

'But you don't work on Saturdays,' Gary objected, patting a vacant stool at the breakfast bar. 'Come and tell me what's put vinegar in your pretty mouth this morning.'

'But I am today,' she countered with heavy, forced patience. 'Special clients get special concessions. Which was one of the too-numerous-to-mention reasons why I didn't want to go to that dreadful party last night.' Which he had conveniently forgotten. He only remembered what he wanted to, and what he had forgotten he made up. Which was what made him such a good reporter, she supposed, earning him his byline with a tabloid which was openly derided and universally read.

'But it was a beautiful party, sweetheart.' Gary's grin threatened to split his face. 'Hannah's agreed to give it another go. We're back together again and—even better—she's going to move in with me. If it works out we're going to make it legal.'

'That's wonderful!' Zoe's small, triangular face warmed into a lovely smile. She had forgotten to be cross. She was generously pleased for him, despite what he had put her through.

During the three years they'd shared this house she had watched the arrivals and departures of Gary's girlfriends with a fairly impartial eye. But Hannah had been special, she had been able to tell that by the way he looked at her, the way he never stopped talking about her. And then there had been the row, the big one. Zoe had never learned the reason, but the upshot had been an abrupt break-off of the relationship. And the upshot of that had been Gary's long face and heartrending sighs, his sudden lack of interest in anything.

And that was why, after a great deal of persuasion, she'd agreed to go to that party. Because he'd begged. It was an annual thing, a fancy dress thrash for the members—and their guests—of the tennis club he'd recently joined because Hannah was a staunch member herself and where she was, Gary needed to be. And if Hannah could see him with another woman—a gorgeous woman—she might just be jealous. And if she was jealous he could work on it, persuade her to come back to him. That had been the theory.

The theme of Tarts and Vicars hadn't appealed, though. Zoe was something of a blue-stocking and not ashamed of it, and she'd spent most of her life being sensible and responsible. So she'd said, 'It won't work. Hannah knows me. I'm your tenant, that's all.' But Gary had had an answer for that.

'Don't you believe it! Hannah never did like the idea of my sharing a pad with two gorgeous females. She was always the teeniest bit miffed by the intimacies she imagined we shared.'

'I suppose I could always go as a Vicar,' Zoe had offered, not seeing herself as the other, and Gary had scorned,

'If you think Hannah will see you as sexy competition dressed up as a clerical gent, you're off your trolley.'

And Jenna, the third inhabitant of the tall, early Victorian brown-brick terraced house, had echoed his scorn.

'You'd defeat the object of the exercise. I'd go myself if I didn't already have a heavy date. It'll be fun, and I'll help you. Make-up, hair, clothes—leave it to me.' As an aspiring actress with her first TV part firmly in her pocket, Jenna exuded the type of confidence that was enough to persuade anyone to do anything.

So Zoe had agreed to go, for the sake of Gary's love-life. He'd been impossible since Hannah had given him the elbow. And even though she'd hated the way Jenna had made her look, she'd decided it might be fun as long as she forgot she was Zoe Kilgerran, one of the junior partners in a firm of big city accountants, responsible, sensible and—let's face it—a tiny bit dull.

'So you'll understand if I ask if you'd share the basement with Jenna? Starting as of today.' Gary put a steaming mug of black coffee into her hands, his face very bland. 'Hannah and I want the house to ourselves. You know how it is ... We want to be able to run around naked if we feel like it, make love on the kitchen table... Anyway, did you get home OK last night?'

'I thought you'd never ask,' Zoe grouched, memories of what had happened to her flooding back. And knowing she was expected to move into the basement flat today didn't help to make her feel any sunnier.

She fully understood Gary's and Hannah's need to have their own space—it looked as if this was the real thing. But Dad was bringing the twins round this afternoon, leaving them with her for the weekend, and the basement flat was small and she'd never get her stuff shifted before they arrived—not with the meeting she had this morning.

Her lower lip jutted pugnaciously.

'I understood why you couldn't escort me home from that party—you'd got it together with Hannah and couldn't give a damn what happened to me——'

'Hang on!' Gary shot her a hurt look which somehow didn't ring true. 'I fixed you a ride home, didn't I?'

'So you did, silly me!' Sarcasm dripped off her tongue. 'With a sex maniac who ended up throwing me out of the car in some godforsaken back street, where I got lectured by some passing do-gooder on the fool-hardiness of my trade! So much better, of course, than my own idea of taking a cab home! And don't you dare laugh!' she shrieked as she saw his mouth twitch. And proceeded to fill him in on the details, which sobered him and enabled her blood-pressure to slide back from danger point.

'I'll kill the creep!' her landlord announced darkly, coming quickly to her side, hugging her. 'He must have had more to drink than I realised. Sober, Dan's OK—a

bit big in the ego department, but fine if you don't try
to cut him down to size. But once he gets a couple of
drinks over the odds inside him he believes he's God's
gift to womankind, or so I'm told. I've never seen that
side of him myself and he seemed sober as a judge when
he told me driving you home wouldn't take him far out
of his way, since he lives in Greenwich. If I'd thought
for one——'

'Forget it. Maybe I'll forgive you in time.' She gave
him a weak smile. The memory of what that whatever
his name was—Dan?—had put her through last night
still made her feel sick inside and she was running late
already. She moved out of his embrace and rallied
enough to toss over her shoulder as she left the room,
'If I move into the basement I'll expect a rent reduction,
and you can do my share of the cleaning for a month
to make up—partly, mind—for what you let me in for
last night!'

But she was back to feeling draggy as she scrambled
as quickly as her sore knees and shins would allow into
one of her severely styled grey business suits and pulled
back her abundant hair into the no-nonsense knot that
made her look older than the teenager her lack of height,
slight build and piquant features sometimes led her to
be taken for.

That man, last night, had formed the impression that
she was a fifteen-year-old prostitute, she remembered,
her pale skin taking fiery embarrassment on board. Her
encounter with him had been even worse than the in-car
scuffle with the creep who had offered to drive her home!
It would be a long time before she forgot his scathing
lecture, the scornful way he had looked her over as she'd
stood in the full glare of his headlights wearing all that
degrading tat!

And even when she'd partially recovered from the combination of shocked outrage and fright he hadn't given her a chance to tell him the truth. He was obviously the sort who formed an opinion and stuck to it, no matter what, because it was his—unable, ever, to concede that he might be wrong!

She ground her teeth as she pushed her feet into the plain black shoes that gave her two extra inches, applied the soft pink lipstick which was all the make-up she usually wore, apart from moisturiser which was a must in the dusty city, and made for the door, determined to put last night's highly embarrassing happenings right out of her mind.

But she should have thanked him, she fretted, as the bus that took her to the centre of the capital jolted through traffic. Heaven only knew what might have happened if he hadn't phoned for transport. She might have had to walk for miles in those silly scarlet heels before she'd found a cruising taxi, and walking through the warren of run-down streets, in that particular area, was not a sensible thing for a lone female to do. Not many men would have stopped to see if she was all right, taking the way she'd been dressed as evidence of her profession and leaving her to get out of a mess which was patently of her own making.

So she should have swallowed her pride and thanked him. But she hadn't, she told herself crossly, and that was the end of it. She would never set eyes on him again and, as from this very moment, she would forget all about the horrible incident. Chewing it over in her mind was a pointless waste of mental energy.

She was later than she'd feared and felt panic squeeze her lungs as she waited for the lift that would take her to the fifth floor of the tower block—all glittering glass and muted silence—to the rooms occupied by Halraike Hopkins. She was never late, she never panicked, and this was an important occasion. As soon as her sister, Petra, took up her new and well-paid job she, Zoe, would be able to afford to move nearer the centre, take a mortgage out on a decent flat of her own and not have to face the awful bus journey from Peckham each morning. She couldn't wait!

But that was in the future and her immediate boss, Luke Taylor, one of the senior partners, would never forgive her if she gave a bad impression—like being un- punctual, hobbling because her scrapes and grazes were giving her gyp, and compounding it all by looking panicky. If he could add the Wright and Grantham ac- count to his portfolio he would be a happy and proud man.

Wright and Grantham, she had no need to remind herself, was a hugely successful drug company and their chief executive, no less, was meeting informally with them this morning to discuss the handling of their ac- counts. Already she was a full fifteen minutes late.

She was beginning to sweat as the lift arrived and she shot into the metal box and punched the button for the fifth floor. She would have had her secretary sit in on the meeting but Luke had stressed that he'd wanted this meeting to be fairly informal. Zoe could make discreet notes herself. He wanted everything nice and smooth and relaxed.

Light years away from feeling anywhere near smooth and relaxed, she limped out of the lift and had to force herself to stand still and try to haul herself together.

Taking slow, deep breaths, she closed her eyes and mentally absorbed the quiet, understated elegance of the vast reception area, the Saturday morning silence broken only by the muted hum of the air-conditioning.

She was good at her job, knew how to handle her team—with firmness but good humour, bringing out the best from them—and was, she knew, a respected employee on a salary many would envy. So she would walk in there and make a serene apology, refer briefly to horrendous traffic conditions, and leave it at that.

Trying to ignore the painful twinges in her legs, she pinned a cool smile on her lips and walked into Luke's office. And nearly died.

CHAPTER TWO

SHE had known she would never forget his face but hadn't realised just how soon it would be proved.

So James Cade, the highly respected and reputedly terrifying chief executive of Wright and Grantham, was the scathing knight-errant who had arbitrarily decided she was a fifteen-year-old hooker!

Cringingly deep embarrassment made her want to slide through the floor and she made her halting apology in a breathy whisper which was so totally unlike her normal cool, collected tone that she felt endlessly ashamed of herself, and Luke's slightly sarcastic, 'So you made it at last,' didn't help and made her go pink right to the tips of her ears.

The two men occupied leather armchairs with a low table between them and perhaps it was the contrast with James Cade's hard, utterly assured confidence that made Luke look wound up to the point of taking off into orbit. At thirty, probably the other man's junior by five years, Luke was already beginning to lose his sandy hair because he worried too much. Worried that in a handful of years' time he would be over the hill, considered too old for original thinking... Worried about the state of his marriage...

'Coffee, Zoe.' Luke's instruction, the laboured tone of his voice, jerked her into showing that she hadn't grown roots into the luxuriously carpeted floor and she hurried, uncomfortably aware that she was hobbling, into his secretaries' office and closed the door far too vigorously behind her, leaning against it for a second to get her breathing back under control and her mind tidily together.

But she couldn't hide forever and so demonstrate to their would-be prestigious new client that she couldn't even produce coffee for three efficiently. Brusquely, she went to work on her mental processes and by the time she had the tray ready she'd convinced herself that, although she might have recognised him immediately—and who the heck wouldn't? He was dauntingly unforgettable—there was no way he would recognise her.

The small, neat, unobtrusively grey personage she projected today was as unlike last night's cleavage-and-fishnet trollop as it was possible to get. He would never in a million years equate a primly understated twenty-five-year-old accountant with a supposedly fifteen-year-old female of the night who got herself flung out of cars by disgruntled customers!

Not allowing herself to dwell overlong on that aspect because if she did she would stay permanently beetroot-coloured, Zoe carried the tray through, placed it neatly on the table, poured, murmured softly about helping themselves to cream and sugar and sat on the third strategically placed and glaringly unoccupied chair and quietly fished her reading glasses and notepad from her handbag.

And only then, when she was neatly settled, did she force herself to look at him. She couldn't stare at the section of wall beyond his impressive, dark-suited shoulders for the entire meeting. He would notice and think she was peculiar.

She didn't want him to have any thoughts about her at all.

There was no doubt about it, she conceded, he was an intensely, formidably attractive specimen. His tall, lean body was clothed with elegant urbanity, the look of complete assurance on his hard-bitten features saved from being awesomely terrifying by the sensual sweep of his wide lower lip.

And Luke was doing all the talking, outlining the comprehensive, confidential and detailed services offered by Halraike Hopkins and she, unprecedentedly, was saying nothing, because if she kept a low enough profile he might forget she was there, and that would be nice, even though she was positively sure he wouldn't recognise her in a month of Sundays.

But he turned his attention from Luke and as she came into the firing line of those chilling grey eyes she wasn't so sure. The look was cold, calculating and very, very comprehensive. He would be difficult, if not impossible, to fool, she thought, gulping, wondering if she should try to display a small, polite smile as his eyes left the soft pink of her mouth and locked on to her apprehensive green eyes.

Luke was still talking and James Cade was still impaling her with those impressively clever eyes and Zoe went hot all over, pushed at her glasses with a nervous finger and tried to convince herself that he couldn't possibly recognise her, trying to see her nondescript appearance through his eyes—the neatly structured, almost mannish grey suit, the tightly confined hair, dark-rimmed spectacles...

As if picking up on her thought processes, his gaze travelled quickly over her body, down to her toes, then swept back up again to dwell on her slender, primly disposed legs.

Could he see those angry-looking grazes and scrapes through the sheer stockings she was wearing? Could he? Her one personal extravagance was pure silk stockings, as light and airy as thistledown. Too late now to wish she'd invested in a few pairs of thick lisle numbers.

Zoe wanted to scream and couldn't remember ever having felt quite so relieved as she did when James Cade eventually rose from his chair with a fluid economy of movement, ending the meeting, his hand outstretched to Luke who had scrambled to his feet.

'Thank you for your time,' Cade said smoothly. 'Get one of your people to set up a meeting with our MD and company accountant at head office and we'll get the ball rolling.'

Thank God it was over, Zoe thought on a wave of weak relief as she pushed herself up out of the low leather chair, unable to hide a wince of pain, and he noted it, of course he did, and his mouth was grim as he held out his hand.

There was no option but to take it and the touch of firm flesh and hard bone as long fingers clasped hers was like nothing that had ever happened to her before. At any moment she could dissolve into the carpet because the simple touch of his hand as it swallowed hers made everything she was made of fall to pieces.

Nerves, she told herself as her boss escorted James Cade out to the lift. She had behaved like a halfwit throughout the short meeting but she refused to blame herself. Who wouldn't have been crippled by nervousness in such circumstances?

But Luke, of course, had no idea of the shock she'd sustained and his, 'Well you were a lot of help!' as he walked back in carried enough censure for the two of them. 'You might have been a pile of bricks for all the input you made. You'll be handling everything from now on. I hope to God you took notes.' Then, with tardy concern, 'You're not feeling ill or anything, are you?'

Stacking the coffee-cups back on the tray, Zoe thought of the indecipherable squiggles on her notepad and shuddered. But she was back in control again, thinking on her feet. She'd get Simon Elliot, her PA, to set the meeting up as quickly as possible, no problem there, and she said sweetly, 'No, I'm fine. You put our case beautifully and I might be wrong but Cade struck me as the type who would prefer any direct dealings to be with another man. I would imagine he has little time for women in the workplace—up there in his rarefied atmosphere, in any case. I imagine he expects women to be seen and not heard, to sit quietly like good little secretaries, take notes and leave the thinking to the big boys.'

He hadn't struck her as any such thing, she simply hadn't thought beyond the dreadful embarrassment of seeing him again. But it was as good an excuse as any to explain the way she'd acted and Luke obviously thought it made sense because he followed as she carried the tray out, ruminating,

'You could be so right. Nice thinking!' He smiled at her suddenly, the worry lines rolling off his forehead. 'He's a cold devil and reputedly doesn't suffer fools at all—let alone gladly. And his reputation with women stinks. Use them and drop them!'

Zoe, rinsing out the cups at the sink in the cubbyhole adjoining the secretaries' office, thought she detected a note of admiration in his voice and fell to wondering if she'd been right to be irritated by his wife's regular phone calls demanding to know where he was, why he was late when he'd said he'd be early, complaining that he'd forgotten he'd promised to attend the children's sports day, end of term play—whatever.

She'd been irritated by Julie Taylor's whining, anxious tone so many times in the past but now she was beginning to feel sorry for her. It just went to reinforce her opinion that it must be awful to become so dependent on a partner. It turned a person into a bag of neuroses, stripped them of their self-respect.

'But he's a clever bastard!' He sounded as if he were verbally rubbing his hands. 'Rumour has it he's about to become engaged to his chairman's daughter. An astute career move, that! He's at the top of his particular tree at the moment; marriage to Stephanie Wright will cement him there permanently.'

'Perhaps they're madly in love with each other,' Zoe said, remembering his awesome good looks, and with a slightly repressive note in her voice because, although all the staff at Halraike Hopkins were properly discreet when with outsiders, gossip tended to get a bit rife internally and she couldn't approve of that.

And Luke drawled back, letting her know just how dull he thought she was, 'Wise up, Zoe. Steph Wright's a first-class bitch. A man would have to be a fool to fall for her. And Cade's far from that.'

Drying her hands, Zoe wondered why she felt so disappointed. A man as charismatic, as obviously intelligent and authoritative as James Cade didn't need to marry for such sordid reasons. He could get wherever he wanted to get under his own steam. But it was none of her business and she didn't care how he conducted his life, of course she didn't. The only thing that could possibly concern her was his lack of recognition of her.

Luke followed her out, locking the communicating door behind him, and as she gathered her bag he suggested, a little too studiously offhand, 'How about a spot of lunch to celebrate? Cade wouldn't have asked for this meeting if he hadn't already gone through our records with a fine-tooth comb and a magnifying glass and decided to use us, we knew that. But it's nice to have everything tied up. It won't hurt for once if you're late getting out to the cottage.'

No wonder his wife never quite knew when to expect him, Zoe decided as she declined his offer coolly.

'I'll have to pass on that. I'm not visiting this weekend. Dad's got a reunion on and Petra's away so he's bringing the twins to me.' She glanced at her plain, serviceable wristwatch. Because of this morning's meeting she wouldn't have been able to get out to the Kent borders in time for her father to set out for Birmingham for the Korean Veterans reunion he looked forward to attending each year. So she would have to cope with the boys here in London. And move her gear into the basement. It was going to be a trying weekend.

She was already later than she'd expected to be and she walked quickly to the door, shaking her head as Luke offered, 'I'll give you a lift, shall I?'

The offer was tempting. It would save time. But if she went to the Elephant and Castle by Underground and then on by bus, she shouldn't keep Dad hanging around for too long. And her new sympathy for Luke's wife wouldn't let her be so selfish so she urged, 'There's really no need, thanks. Get back to Julie and the kids; there's still plenty of weekend left if you don't waste it.'

But the look on his face told her that a celebratory lunch with a colleague would have been more to his liking than mowing the lawn or taking his family shopping. And it reinforced her long-held opinion that going solo was much safer than pairing up. You could always rely on yourself but rarely on anyone else. Anyone else could lose interest, grow away. Or just plain die. Or let you believe things that simply weren't true.

In the event she wasn't late at all and was hurrying as best she could down the street when she saw her father's ancient Ford estate pull up in front of the house she shared.

Suddenly overwhelmed by fondness for him, she swallowed the lump in her throat and put her feeling of vulnerability down to the traumas and mortifications of last night and this morning. It wasn't like her to get needlessly tearful, or sentimental, but she couldn't help thinking that he deserved better from life than what he had.

They had been such a close and happy family, her father, mother, Petra and herself. And Rufus, the dog. All squashed together in the two-bedroomed cottage just inside Kent and loving it, not yearning for anything bigger and better because they all had each other and nothing else really counted.

Until fourteen years ago when her mother had died and the light had gone out of everything. Zoe had felt betrayed. It had seemed, for a time, as if her whole world was falling apart, but her father had made sure it hadn't.

He had said goodbye to his hopes of a headship and had taught part-time so he could be with his daughters, until his voluntary retirement two years ago. Which had meant, of course, that money had been in short supply and he'd had to make sacrifices most other men would have refused to do.

He had adored his wife and he'd never got over her early death and, although he'd always done his best to disguise his pain, to make their home life as happy and normal as possible, he hadn't been able to hide the hurt in his eyes, at least not from Zoe.

And because Petra had only just turned eight when their mother had died Zoe had gallantly tried to take her place, becoming responsible and preternaturally sensible in her efforts to help her father carry on as if everything was all right.

Forcing the bleak and thankfully rare mood of introspection away, she pinned on a smile and went to give her father a hug as he tugged the bags of baby impedimenta out of the boot. A big-boned man, he was beginning to stoop, and the hair which had turned grey in the months following the death of his devotedly loved wife was going thin on top. Swallowing an inner pang, she made her smile wider.

'You look very smart, Dad.' And he did. The grey flannels he wore were immaculately pressed and his old regimental badge looked impressive on his dark blazer. 'I'm sorry you had to go to the trouble of bringing the babies out here.'

'Don't be silly.' His kind eyes smiled down into hers as he turned from stacking the last bag neatly on the pavement. 'You had a meeting and your career's more important than my trip to Birmingham.'

She wanted to tell him it wasn't, not really, that he had more than earned just one weekend for himself out of fifty-two. But she didn't because he simply wouldn't see it that way. Ever since the death of his wife his daughters had come first, their happiness and emotional security his prime concern.

Which was why, two years ago when the twins had been a few months old, he had taken early retirement in order to help look after them because Petra had been busy pushing herself through her Open University course.

And, if he hadn't been unable to stop loving his wife, grieving for her, then he would have remarried at some stage, concentrating on his career and handing over the responsibility of caring for his two daughters and, later, his small grandsons.

But now wasn't the time to stand around as if she were in a dream, allowing her mind to backtrack through the years. Dad had a long drive ahead of him.

Gathering herself, she opened the rear car door and Bill Kilgerran said, 'Gently. They're both asleep.'

But just beginning to wake, she noted, going gooey as always when they were like this: two identical boneless blond puddings, long lashes fluttering over flushed cheeks. Blessedly quiet, just for the moment!

They each unstrapped a twin from an identical car seat and just before small chubby arms put a stranglehold on her neck Zoe saw hers was Robin. He had a brown fleck in the iris of one of his big blue eyes. Rickie didn't, which was kind of Mother Nature as it stopped them getting muddled up completely.

The little boy nuzzled his cheek against hers and she gave herself a moment of auntly joy as she cuddled him back and then got into brisk and sensible mode, reached for one of the lined-up bags with her free hand and went carefully up the steps and into the house.

The long narrow hall already seemed to be full of luggage—suitcases, things in boxes, a portable TV. Hannah. Of course! Her slight frown was in danger of becoming a full-blown scowl so she straightened her brow, put Robin on his feet, took Rickie from her father, gave him a quick cuddle and set him down beside his twin.

Following her father back down the steps, she gathered the remainder of the twins' bits and pieces and told him,

'Don't hang around. If you try to make up lost time on the motorway that old rattletrap will fall to pieces.'

She was doing it again! she thought, mentally shaking her head at herself. For the past fourteen years, one way or another, she'd been trying to be the little mother, fussing and worrying, taking her self-inflicted responsibilities far too much to heart—not that it had prevented what had happened to Petra...

'Don't cast aspersions—she might hear, go into one of her sulks and refuse to start at all!' Bill Kilgerran brushed a knuckled fist lightly over his daughter's pointed chin and added with a smile that hid the wryness, 'When you learn to stop fretting I'll throw a party. Now, if the boys get too rumbustious, take them for a long walk. It works like a dream. And I'll be back here tomorrow afternoon to pick them up.'

Which gave her something else to fret about, because every year he stayed for the reunion weekend with his old friend from National Service days. Jack Foster and his wife Elaine lived in the Birmingham suburb of Solihull and after the reunion dinner and dance they had Sunday to get over it, plenty of things to reminisce about, to catch up on over a pint at the local, followed by one of Elaine's apparently memorable Sunday roasts.

But Dad would have to miss out on his relaxing full day with his friend, Zoe thought regretfully, waving until he rounded the corner. But they had both agreed that Petra needed the break...

Suddenly aware that the household behind her was ominously quiet, she made her sore legs carry her up the steps at a run. And she had been right in guessing there was mischief afoot because both the tiny boys were practically upended in one of Hannah's boxes, unpacking the contents with mountains of glee and little method.

'No! Naughty!' she admonished as sternly as she could, hooking an arm round each small body and hauling them out, rescuing a coat hanger from Rickie's clinging fingers just as Hannah and Gary came slowly down the stairs, breathing hard, carrying the dressing-table from what had been Zoe's room between them.

Halfway down they stopped for a breather and Hannah poked her rumpled head over the banisters.

'Gary said you were looking after your sister's kids this weekend so we thought we'd help move your stuff.' She smiled shyly. 'I hope you don't mind, but...' Her voice tailed off and Zoe took up,

'But you want me out of the way, shut away in the basement so you two can play house.' The smile in her voice robbed her words of any sting and the boys began to race round the hall on sturdy legs, chortling like wild things. The 'bumping from stair to stair' downward progress of the dressing-table had kept them quiet and enthralled but the journey had come to a standstill, and that was boring.

But the sudden eruption of Jenna into the hall, clad in what appeared to be a gauzy patterned throwover shirt and nothing else, closely followed by a tall, lanky guy who had to be the actress's newest date, had them scampering for safety, clinging, shyly burying their flushed faces in Zoe's skirt.

The sooner she changed into a pair of old jeans, the better, Zoe thought, absently patting two lint-blond heads, though how that would be accomplished when her possessions appeared to be in transit, with a goodly proportion wedged permanently on the stairs, she had no idea. She was beginning to get a headache.

She smiled tentatively at the lanky guy who smiled warily back. And Jenna crooned, 'Zoe, my pet—meet

Henry.' She stroked the side of his lean face lingeringly.
'Isn't he gorgeous? I do believe I might marry him. At
least,' she batted fabulous lashes, 'I shall move in with
him to avoid having to share that meagre basement. No
offence, Zoe, my pet—but really! Oi, you two,' she
hollered up the staircase. 'Come down at once. I want
your opinion.'

A distracted grunt was the only reply and Zoe wondered just what was going on behind that dressing-table,
and Jenna patted Henry's backside lovingly, ordering,
'Do lend a hand, otherwise they'll be there all day.'

It's a madhouse, Zoe thought, subsiding on to the hall
chair, feeling hot and bothered in her neat office gear
as the midsummer sun poured in through the open hall
door.

She dragged the twins up on her lap, out of the way,
as Henry took one end of the recalcitrant piece of furniture and began to tug and Jenna shouted above the
din.

'My lovely room will look like a used furniture em-
porium! How much more do you think you'll try to fit
in?' But the furniture removers ignored her and Zoe
wondered whether to tell her not to worry because any
time now she would be moving out herself, just as soon
as she'd finished saving for a deposit on a place of her
own. Now that Petra had a well paid job to go to, she
would be able to afford it.

She closed her eyes briefly, picturing it—somewhere
fairly central, peaceful, a place for everything and
everything in its place, nothing pandemonic about it—
and the moment had gone. No chance to tell Jenna anything as the dressing-table came to rest at the foot of the
stairs and the actress clapped her hands and commanded,
'Gather round folks, I want advice.'

Henry dusted off his hands and the upward drift of his wide bony shoulders seemed to say, She's impossible, but cute. Then Hannah and Gary emerged, their hands twined together, and Hannah, despite the wildness of her curly dark hair, looked cool and lovely in brief lemon-yellow shorts which showed off her endless legs and a skimpy sleeveless top.

'Right!' Jenna flashed her wide white smile when she had their undivided attention. 'You know about my part in this TV drama, and I guess I have to concede it's only walk on, walk off and half a dozen tiny words. But I aim to make a big impression, folks! So I've got to look *re-all-y*——' she spun the word out '—sexy, with a capital S. I appear at a poolside, right? I think I look sexier with this cover-up——' she tweaked the edges of the diaphanous shirt '—sort of alluring—some mystery, you know.' Briefly, she paraded up and down the cluttered limits of the hall. 'But Henry here says it's better without——' She stopped, shrugging out of the filmy shirt, holding her arms dramatically wide, revealing ripely voluptuous curves in a bikini so small it was barely there. 'So——?' she questioned breathlessly. 'What do you guys think?'

Catcalls and whistles, someone—probably Gary—was stamping his feet, and Zoe closed her eyes and wished she could close her ears, too, to shut out the din, and wished she had never been born when that unmistakable voice said with the cool precision she was beginning to dread, 'I have no wish to sound offensive, but don't you think your activities should be conducted more discreetly?'

The sudden strained silence made Zoe's heart pound. She went hot all over, perspiration soaking the neat white blouse she wore beneath her suit jacket. It took a lot of courage to turn her head. Slowly.

James Cade was standing in the open hall doorway, impeccably suited against the background of the dusty street. Cool, collected and in control. Utterly. Dominating his audience.

The austerely beautiful features betrayed nothing, not a thing, not even disdain, and the cold grey eyes took in every single thing, labelling it, filing it away inside that clever brain. Everything. Jenna, posing, unashamedly near-naked; Gary and Hannah clinging together, one of Gary's hands, shocked by the disruptive advent of the stranger to complete immobility, curving around Hannah's pert breast; the clutter, the unbelievable clutter—boxes and bags, the abandoned dressing-table leaning drunkenly against one wall.

'Want something?' Gary was the first to recover. His hand slid down to Hannah's waist and his jaw was belligerent. 'You're on private property.'

'As your antics are clearly visible from the street I imagined privacy was the last thing you bothered about.' James Cade was visibly unimpressed by Gary's pugnacious stance. His hands were thrust negligently into the trouser pockets of the superbly tailored lightweight suit he wore and, with the sunlight behind him, his features were more darkly dangerous than even Zoe remembered them.

Her arms tightened around the twins and she shivered. And the shiver turned into a shudder that went soul-deep as the voice that was insolent in its coolness imparted, 'I want a private word with Miss Kilgerran.'

Unaware of the questioning look Gary shot in her direction, Zoe gulped. She couldn't believe this was happening. She shook her head, hoping he'd disappear.

But he didn't. He had tracked her down and there could be only one reason for that.

He recognised her from the night before. She hadn't really believed it possible.

One of the twins was pulling the pins out of her hair and it fell down around her face like a shiny blonde cloud and she gasped out the first thing that came into her head.

'How did you know where I lived?'

A silly thing to say, she realised belatedly. She, who had never said a silly thing in her life, had spoken as if she had something to hide.

'The usual channels,' he answered with cool menace, advancing further into the cluttered hall, picking his way round a pile of toys that had spilled from one of the carriers.

Whatever that meant, Zoe thought and closed her eyes in complete despair as Gary, as if satisfied that she and James Cade knew each other, draped an arm round Hannah's waist and said leeringly, 'Right, folks—bed now. Everyone upstairs on the double! Let's get at it!'

I'll strangle him! I will, I will! Zoe thought, horribly close to a state of hysteria for the first time in her life. She didn't know about Henry, but the others all took life and sex so lightheartedly, making a joke out of nearly everything, batting sexual innuendoes around like tennis balls in the Wimbledon finals. They were going to shift her bed down to the basement. She knew that. James Cade wouldn't. He would think the whole household was set for an orgy!

Both the little boys were squirming around on her lap, babbling about biscuits which meant it was way past their lunchtime, and Zoe couldn't have got to her feet if she'd wanted to because even if her legs hadn't turned to water the twins were pinning her down. And James Cade clipped derisively, 'Does Taylor know about the double life you lead? Is he a dupe, or do you give him a few favours on the side to keep him quiet? I hear his marriage is shaky and now I understand why.'

There was no expression on his hard features and that, somehow, was worse than a sneer. How could he imply she and Luke...? How could he believe she was—what he thought she was?

Violent denials exploded in her brain, denials she was unable to put into coherent words. Not that he gave her the opportunity because he just stood there, feet planted apart, telling her exactly what she didn't want to hear.

'When you walked in this morning I knew I'd seen you before. When I noticed the fresh grazes on your legs the penny dropped. But I didn't fully believe it until I walked in on this sordid set-up.' A nerve jumped at the side of his tense jawline and then cold grey eyes swept over the restless twins. The family likeness was unmissable. 'Yours. Why, I wonder, do I find myself so unamazed?' He rocked back on his heels. 'Do you know who the father is?'

Grey eyes impaled her, as if drilling deep inside her brain and, her mind an impossible jumble of repudiations and denials, she squeakily told the truth.

'No.'

Petra had adamantly refused to tell anyone the identity of the man who had used her and dropped her, doing a vanishing act the moment he'd learned she was pregnant. And Zoe had told the truth because her mind was direct. She didn't stall or bend the facts to suit the circumstances and had blown her chance to explain that the twins weren't hers, because he turned smartly on his heels and walked straight out.

CHAPTER THREE

'THE restaurant's in Fallow Street—can you find your own way there? Or shall I send a car?' The dark voice was even more curt this morning, but Zoe was too relieved to hear it to care.

'Twelve-thirty, Mr Cade; I'll be there. And of course I can make my own way.' She was practically burbling.

'I've no doubt you can,' he came back drily, and before she could work out what that tone was supposed to mean the line went dead.

Replacing the receiver, she glanced at her watch. Lunch with James Cade in exactly one hour. She grinned. Exhilaration got her bouncing to her feet, far too unsettled now to continue with the particularly knotty set of profit and loss sheets she'd been working on.

The weekend had been far from relaxing. What with having to move into the basement rooms with a miffed Jenna who kept muttering darkly about going to live in sin with Henry, caring for two energetic small boys who obviously thought that aunts were people who had nothing else to do but play with them and allow them to eat chocolate bars instead of lunch, and agonising over James Cade's totally unexpected and incomprehensible arrival—and abrupt departure, on such a deeply embarrassing note, too—she had entered Monday morning feeling frayed to the point of disintegration.

And hadn't been able to concentrate properly on her work, either, because her mind had kept sliding off at a tangent, grappling with the problem of how on earth she could approach James Cade and put him right.

What he privately thought of her morals was neither here nor there; she accepted that. After all, her company would be working for his company and that was as far as their relationship would go. And the only time that they ever need meet would be for a short session before she tackled his personal tax returns and his no doubt massive portfolio of investments.

But the knowledge that he thought she was some sort of Jekyll and Hyde character, doing a bit of hookering in her spare time, sharing a house with what he had probably decided were pimps and their prospects and already having two small sons—and no idea who their father was—was too awful to live with!

So his unexpected invitation to lunch was the answer to her prayers, and then some! And Zoe felt completely cheerful and nicely in control again for the first time since that awful fancy dress party on Friday night.

She poked her head into the adjoining office, checked that Simon, her PA, had set up the initial formal meeting with Wright and Grantham and had the final audit for Future Computers well in hand, told her secretary that she would be out of the office for a couple of hours, then retreated into her own office, collected her washbag from her desk and tripped light-heartedly to the ladies' room.

Hanging her suit jacket and crisp white blouse on the hooks on the inside of the door, she uncapped the gel she preferred to wash with and vigorously sluiced her face with warm water.

Cade had almost certainly set up this meeting to fill her in on his personal tax details—handling all the director's returns would come within her brief—because he wasn't a fool. While she and her team would do all the hard graft, Luke, as the senior partner, would pick up the credit. James Cade would know that and would want, initially anyway, to liaise with her directly. And she would take the heaven-sent opportunity to explain that his warped opinion of her was completely and utterly incorrect.

Because, far from being sexually promiscuous, she had never had a lover in her life. One or two boyfriends, that was all, and they had been politely given the heave-ho when they had tried to get too fresh or too serious.

But she wouldn't tell him that, of course; her hang-ups were her own business. Not that they were exactly that, she assured herself as she smoothed moisturiser into her fine, pale skin. She preferred to think of her celibate state as a well-rationalised decision, arrived at after sensibly weighing the pros and cons.

She had first-hand evidence of how loving could destroy a person. And, quite apart from not wanting to take the risk of that happening to her, she valued her freedom and independence. She had worked hard to attain it and didn't intend to lose it.

Zoe buttoned herself into her blouse and shrugged into her lightweight suit jacket. So far, so good. Not one strand of blonde hair escaping the pins that held it in its neat knot, her small features serene, only the sparkle in her big green eyes betraying her pleasant anticipation of the coming meeting.

An anticipation that was solely down to the comforting knowledge that before lunch was over James Cade would have revised his embarrassing opinion of her, she assured herself as she opted to walk to the restaurant he had named. The spring in her step had nothing to do with the man himself, his undoubtedly awesome good looks, his sheer mind-blowing presence.

Forcing herself to slow down her pace because if she kept bouncing along in the warm June sun she would arrive looking hot and sweaty, she found her thoughts unaccountably turning to the woman Cade was to marry.

And she knew, with a feminine intuition that rather surprised her, that Stephanie Wright would have to be a very strong lady indeed to be able to handle the almost frightening maleness of Cade. He would walk all over a weak woman, dominate her utterly—and probably end up despising her.

She had never met his chairman's daughter and wasn't likely to, but she could paint pictures in her head of someone very glossy, smoothly sophisticated and tough. She would have to be, to have attracted a man like Cade. And, being tough, the likes of Luke Taylor would label her 'bitch' because men disliked strong women more often than not; they made them feel insecure so they called them names to make them feel better themselves.

James Cade was the type who would respect a strong woman, consider her his equal. So he wouldn't be contemplating marriage to cement his career, she decided cosily; he was probably deeply in love with his Stephanie.

And quite why that neatly worked out snippet should take all her breath away, suddenly drain the bounce out of her step, was something she had no time to work out, because she had arrived. And stood still for a single second while she straightened her suit jacket, hauled back her shoulders, arranged what she hoped was a serene expression on her face and walked on in.

He was already waiting, and as the waiter ushered her to the secluded table for two he rose courteously to his feet and she felt herself go decidedly pink. And knew why. All those dreadful—but understandable, given the circumstances—misconceptions of his!

Which she now had the perfect opportunity to put right, she reassured herself. Zoe the part-time hooker would soon be a thing of the past!

'Thank you for giving me your time,' he said tonelessly, his eyes half hidden beneath heavy lids and an even heavier fringe of thick black lashes.

She didn't think he was actually seeing her at all and Zoe bit back the outrageous impulse to drawl right back, 'I don't give and I don't come cheap. Fifty quid an hour's the going rate,' and wondered if ladies of that sort charged by the hour or by the—— And felt herself go scarlet and wondered just what it was about this man that made her lose all her sanity and say and think the silliest things...

He was towering above her and, all around her, the atmosphere seemed to crackle. He looked mean and moody and, yes, it had to be faced, terrifyingly desirable.

Zoe sat quickly, her breath all gone again, and watched as he seated himself and beckoned a waiter. And that initial show of courtesy wasn't in evidence as he ordered for both of them—bottled mineral water and a plain green salad as it turned out—when for all he knew she might have craved a large gin and a thick rare steak!

Not that she did, of course, it was the principle that counted. But she hadn't come here for the food, she reminded herself, and, looking at things from his viewpoint, he wouldn't consider the type of female he believed her to be deserved much in the way of polite behaviour.

So now was the time, before they got into business discussions, to put him straight. She opened her mouth to do just that but he cut across her, his dispassionate tone more chilling than it had any right to be.

'Before I approach your superiors I think it's only fair to tell you that I intend to have you taken off the Wright and Grantham account.'

'You can't mean that!' Her head felt as if it were about to spin off her shoulders and the fork she'd been holding fell from her fingers and she didn't even notice. Her career prospects with Halraike Hopkins would bite the dust and she would be suspect from here on in. Influential clients didn't make such requests without good reason.

'I don't say things I don't mean.'

To give him his due, he remained silent while the watchful waiter removed the fallen fork and replaced it with another and then he explained, with the softness of a cobra striking.

'But I prefer to look a person in the eye instead of pushing the knife in between the shoulder-blades. Hence this meeting.'

'Oh, but you can't!' Zoe insisted frantically, sliding down in her seat a little because one glance from those coldly, quellingly authoritative grey eyes would have stopped a manic axe-murderer in his tracks.

But he merely contradicted, 'I can. And I will.' He began eating his salad with no sign of enjoyment, as if it was every responsible person's duty to fuel the body so that it could function properly, no more than that.

Zoe couldn't even look at hers and stared at him, knowing she just had to look stupid but unable to do anything about it as he expounded, 'Your morals, or lack of them, are your business, of course. I don't presume to judge——'

'You don't! You, you——' she spluttered, the blistering words that would put him right on that score crowding on the edge of her tongue.

But he silenced her with another killingly quelling look and cut in quietly, 'Normally, no. But what I witnessed late on Friday night, coupled with the fact that you admit you have no idea who the father of your children is—plus the way you appear to live—adds up to the unpleasant truth that your integrity has to be in question. No, hear me out——' He sliced through her hiss of outrage, his voice like ice-edged steel. 'Wright and Grantham's accounts contain certain sensitive information.' He laid down his cutlery and leaned back in his chair, long fingers absently curved around his glass of iced water. 'Our research funding, for example. Which new and possibly revolutionary drugs are being given priority by our research department. All useful information to rival companies. Added to which, you have a useful pusher to hand. The reporter—I thought I recognised him and subsequent checking proved me right—the guy who was so anxious to get everyone in bed. All in the same bed? Or hasn't the depravity gone that far yet?' One dark, well-defined brow rose in a query that was entirely without humour. 'Be that as it may, the information in the wrong hands—his hands and, by implication, yours—could do Wright and Grantham a whole load of no good at all.'

'But I wouldn't!' Zoe exploded, all thoughts of telling him she wasn't the sleazy tramp of his imaginings melting away in the fiery fury of hearing her professional integrity called into question.

Infuriatingly, he shrugged, wide shoulders moving just slightly beneath that smooth, expensive suiting. 'Perhaps, perhaps not. Who's to tell? However——' he dropped his napkin on the table, making it clear the unpleasant interview was at an end '—I am not prepared to take the chance.'

Her brain was reeling. She felt as if she'd just gone ten rounds with a prize fighter. Punch drunk. But she had to pull herself together before he paid the bill and left her staring into a plate of salad and an impoverished future.

Trying to pretend that her face wasn't scarlet with temper, she pushed out her pointy chin and, unaware of the threatening, deep green glitter of her narrowed eyes, told him, 'Before you shoot your mouth off one more time, you can at least give me the chance to explain.' And, ignoring the shutters of boredom that came down over his fascinating eyes, she spelled out the events which had led to her being tipped out of that car, ending with, 'And Rickie and Robin are my nephews. Petra, my sister, is away on a walking holiday in Greece with friends. Dad and I had to practically twist her arm to make her go. She's been working flat-out to get her Open University degree and she needed the break before taking up her job with a literary agency based in Bromley. And, before you start accusing me of lying, no, we don't know who the father is.' Realising that her normally cool, restrained voice had risen to fishwife levels, she took a deep breath and allowed her eyes to leave his, staring instead at the bread roll she'd put on her side plate and hadn't touched.

She began to rip it to shreds.

'Four years ago, when Petra was eighteen,' she explained more calmly, 'she worked as a receptionist in a small hotel near Orpington. Just temporarily, until she took her place at university. Dad's always insisted that we both cram in as much education as possible—he was a teacher.'

For the first time, a tiny smile played round the edges of her mouth, and then she, in turn, shrugged. 'She was looking forward to it, to getting her degree and making a career—with books—in publishing or with an agency. Then she met someone. He swept her off her feet, as the saying goes.' She gave him another shrug, a look that said she didn't believe in that sort of thing herself, and ploughed straight on. 'I was studying hard for my finals at that time, at university myself, so I didn't know what was going on. But Dad knew something was up. Petra stopped going home, and when she did put in an appearance she acted strangely. Then the truth came out. She was pregnant. The creep had talked about marriage, talked about undying love—and she had believed him.' Unconsciously, her voice hardened. 'When he learned she was pregnant, instead of naming the day he told her he was already married with three children. She never saw him again.'

'And she didn't say who he was?' Cade asked, his dry tone telling her he had difficulty believing any of this.

And Zoe came back firmly, 'No. After she broke the news she refused to talk about him. She probably could have traced him and demanded some kind of financial support but she obviously wanted to forget him, put it all behind her. And Dad and I supported her in that.'

'I would imagine the advent of twins made forgetting him a touch difficult.' An unforgivable trace of humour quirked his long mouth, drawing her startled attention to all that latent sensuality.

She would have liked to hit him but controlled herself and said primly, 'None of us has ever looked on the boys as belonging to anyone but our family. We all love them devotedly. Dad helps Petra look after them during the week while I go down to the cottage at weekends to do my bit and give Dad a breathing space. Nobody resents them; we love them to pieces.'

'You haven't once mentioned your mother in all of this.' The new, lighter tone of query in his voice, the careful way he was watching her, gave her hope that he was beginning to believe her at last.

So the relief of that gentled her tone as she told him softly, 'Mum died fourteen years ago. Dad brought us up.'

He had devoted his life to his daughters because with the death of his wife there had been nothing else to live for. And although she could understand such depth of devotion she couldn't condone it. If he had been able to find a new love and marry again—without feeling he was betraying everything he and Mum had been to each other—then he needn't have sacrificed his career in the way he had, and she needn't have had to witness those rare unguarded moments when his deep loneliness had shown in his eyes.

'So your father is left with the unenviable task of bringing up a second family—virtually single-handed if I read you right—as a result of his daughter's thoughtless lack of control.'

Pompous, pious, ignorant bastard!

Zoe ground her teeth, biting back the verbal brickbats she was itching to throw at him, remembering his threats, his ability—if he so chose—to put her prospects within her company at very grave risk.

It wasn't like that. Petra had been deceived in the vilest way possible. Her heart had been broken because she'd loved the man and had believed he loved her, too. Her life could have been ruined but she'd been too strong-willed to let that happen and she, Zoe, and Dad, had been right behind her decision to carry on with her pregnancy.

They'd put their heads together and worked everything out. Petra would get her degree through the Open University and Dad would take early retirement when the babies needed more time-consuming attention, leaving their mother free to push on with her studies.

And Zoe was able to give practical help, too. Visiting every weekend to give a hand, giving all the financial support she could afford because although the state helped it was a pittance and didn't go anywhere. And how dared he imply that all responsibility had been offloaded on to Dad? And the tiny boys didn't represent an 'unenviable task'—they were a joy!

Stormy green eyes clashed with his. She could see the cold condemnation in his eyes and knew she had to allow herself the luxury of putting him in his place. After all, his reasons for wanting her taken off the Wright and Grantham account were no longer valid, he could hardly demand her removal for being less than boot-licking, could he?

'Have you always been so moralistic and judgemental, Mr Cade?' she enquired in the coolest, most dismissive tone she could find. 'Was it something that happened, or were you born like it?' She reached for her handbag, determined that she would be the one to end what had turned out to be a very distasteful, unsettling interview. 'Did you never do something you later regretted when you were an inexperienced eighteen?'

But James Cade would have been born with all the experience in the world buried deep in his frigid soul, she scorned as she gathered herself to go. She couldn't imagine him ever being vulnerable, open to hurt and betrayal. Yet the look in his eyes told her she had inadvertently touched a raw nerve, revived something, a memory perhaps, that he could hardly bear to look at.

Interesting.

Too interesting to share, obviously. His face went blank again, his voice almost soft as he commanded, 'Sit down. I haven't finished with you yet.'

So she did, with a flurry of internal exasperation. She was going to have to watch her tongue. The more time she spent with him, the more she found herself spoiling for a fight. He was, she decided, infinitely dangerous to her equanimity—never mind her sanity!

'I'm sorry.' She arranged her features primly, a slightly off-balance semblance of her normal serene and unflustered expression. 'I thought everything had been resolved.' Perhaps he did want to talk about his personal tax returns, she thought. She couldn't think of anything else he might need to say on the once vexed subject of her suspect morals.

Or maybe, she wondered without a lot of hope, he wanted to apologise. And just stared at him, unable to believe this was happening when he stated coldly,

'I'm still trying to decide—given what you've told me—whether you are as brave and unselfish as you'd like to have me believe, or an accomplished liar.' He settled his elbows on the arm-rests of his chair, grey eyes impaling her above steepled fingers. 'The way you choose to conduct your life doesn't affect me, personally, so don't accuse me of taking the moralistic stance. But your lifestyle could leave you open to blackmail; I'm sure you're intelligent enough to see that. And, as I said, there is a certain amount of sensitive, highly confidential information that our rivals would willingly pay substantial sums to obtain, or certain questionable newspapers would love to use as sensational headline material. "New Wonder Drug—Cure All or Kill All"—I'm sure you can visualise the type of thing?' He allowed his voice to tail off, as if the final word had been said and the subject wearied him, and Zoe sucked in her breath, desperately fighting to find all the control she'd always had at the end of her neat fingers and now seemed to have lost.

And her struggle for composure must have been written all over her face because he lowered his hands and smiled. And the effect was utterly, unnervingly devastating. Made her almost forget his damning opinion of her, his stubborn refusal to believe in her integrity, until he said, 'You don't need to try so hard to project a meek, prim image, Miss Kilgerran. I've seen you in quite a different persona, remember? Black fishnet—a little torn around the knees, but fetching for all that. A cleavage any Page Three girl would be proud of and an apology for a skirt that defies description. And in any case, Miss Kilgerran, your eyes give you away. They positively spit with wild green passion whenever I say something you don't want to hear.'

Oh, the hateful, sarcastic, wicked swine! She would like to take that evil smile and wrap it round his neck until it choked him!

'I've already explained how I came to be dressed that way, Mr Cade.' She marvelled, she really did, at the polite tone she achieved when every mental tooth was grinding down to mental gums. 'And you only need to do some of that checking up you seem so extraordinarily good at to get at the truth regarding the parentage of the twins. Petra is due home on Wednesday, but if you'd rather not wait that long I'm sure my father would be delighted to have you call on him and to answer all the questions you want to ask.'

So get round that, she fulminated, keeping very still because if she allowed herself to move an inch she'd be over the table and thrusting her wretched, untouched salad down his throat, plate as well.

He actually had the gall to shrug, beckon for the bill, hand over his plastic and settle back in his chair. Only then did he bother to look at her, pick up on her suggestion. And he didn't need actually to yawn to underline his boredom. It was all in his tone as he drawled, 'Now why should I do that? You would only need to leave the children with your father, prime him. I'm sure he wouldn't want to see his daughter's well-paid job in jeopardy. After all, what do a few lies matter when hard cash is involved?'

Zoe stared at him, her soft pink mouth open. He was replacing his plastic in his wallet and, clearly, for him, there was nothing more to say on the subject.

Then everything inside her went haywire and nothing mattered at all except the gross and flagrant injustice of it all. She scrambled to her feet and, planting her small fists on the table, ground out, 'There's one sure way you can prove I've been telling the truth, you pious rat! Take me to bed and find out the hard way just how virginal I am!'

CHAPTER FOUR

Zoe couldn't believe it of herself! How could she have said such a thing? Oh, how could she?

James Cade already believed she was completely devoid of morals and integrity and now he would think she'd been propositioning him!

It didn't bear thinking about, but she couldn't get the incident out of her head and every time her office door opened, the phone rang on her desk, she mentally cringed because she was sure it would be a summons to Above where she would be asked if she knew why the chief executive of Wright and Grantham had demanded her removal from their account.

But it never was, and two whole days had gone by and the thunderbolt hadn't dropped. And the first formal meeting with W. and G.'s managing director and company accountant had been fixed for the end of the week and Zoe was going out of her mind.

Cade hadn't believed her explanations. He wouldn't believe Christmas fell in December if he didn't want to. He thought she was as sexually discreet as an alley cat and more than capable of selling his firm's most sensitive secrets to the highest bidder.

So he had no reason to forget his threat. More reason to carry it out because of the way she'd suggested she share his bed!

She went hot all over at the very idea and a sensation that was startlingly new to her—and not exactly unpleasant—made her insides twist up into knots and her legs go weak at the knees.

Not that she'd meant it, of course. Heaven forbid! It was simply that James Cade had the power to affect her brain, turning that normally cool and precise organ into a good imitation of a pan of boiling, seething, hissing spaghetti!

Her legs wobbled precariously as she made her way from the computer station to her desk and picked up the phone with that all too familiar sinking sensation of impending doom inside her and the breath in her lungs turned to a lump of stone as Cade said softly—too softly?—'On further consideration, I'll take you up on your offer.'

'I'm sorry?' she got out at last in strangled tones. Did he really mean what she thought he meant? Oh, this couldn't be happening to her! What had she ever done to deserve it? He had decided to do what she had so madly suggested and put her virginity to the test, the louse!

'You heard,' he said complacently, and Zoe's brick-red face went a painful shade of white.

She had tossed down the gauntlet and he was picking it up. And it was all his fault. She rarely, if ever, lost her temper. She was too level-headed. And she never, but never, said stupid, unforgivable things! And he, and he alone, had made her do just that!

'Lost for words?' There was a bite behind the mockery. 'I'll pick you up at seven, outside your home. Unless,' he suggested with silky menace, 'the point you offered to make is unprovable.'

Oh, the bastard! And what would his nearly-fiancée think of such lousy behaviour? The hypocrite! Accusing her of having fewer morals than she had heads then deciding, no doubt on a whim, to go right ahead and conduct this sexual experiment with a woman he hardly knew and most certainly didn't like or respect.

Groping for her dignity, she caught it, held it, and managed loftily, 'I won't go to bed with you, Mr Cade.' And felt herself drown in confusion as a much too vivid mind picture of the two of them together, naked limbs entwined in a cocoon of silken sheets, presented itself with shocking clarity. And heard him say, through the fiery embarrassment of her shamelessly wayward thoughts.

'I wasn't asking you to, Miss Kilgerran.' There was borderline amusement there somewhere and she felt her body begin to cringe, to shrink away at the definitely pointed put-down. 'You offered to let me speak to your father, remember? You said he'd convince me where you had signally failed. My judgement tells me the Miss Goody-Two-Shoes image is highly suspect, but I have to be sure there's no chance of an injustice before I approach your superiors. So, seven this evening?' And then, as she made a noise of strangled, reluctant assent, he flayed her with scornful arrogance. 'If the time ever came when I did want to go to bed with you, I would. You wouldn't stand a chance, make no mistake about that, Miss Kilgerran.'

And for long, desperately shame-filled moments she stared at the now silent receiver before replacing it.

Her hand shook, she noted abstractedly. She was shaking all over. James Cade had the power to turn her into a gibbering wreck. She wanted to crawl under her desk and never come out.

She had completely and utterly forgotten she'd suggested he talk to her father, let him state which of his daughters had given birth to the twins. All she'd been able to think about was the shocking challenge she'd flung at him.

And that, and that alone, was responsible for the way she'd repeatedly found her mind straying to disgraceful images of a big double bed, sweat-slicked naked bodies— hers and his—writhing limbs, clinging mouths and—— Oh, my gosh, she was doing it again!

Zoe covered her burning face with her hands and gave a heartrending groan. She had to pull herself together. She couldn't go on like this. She only had to think of him to get a rush of sex to the brain. And that wasn't like her at all.

Most women he met would weave dark fantasies around him, she could quite see that. She wasn't blind or stupid. But she wasn't most women. She had no desire to be dominated, in bed or out of it, and she had even less desire to have a lover dangerous enough to force her to surrender to her own sexuality.

But she wasn't going to think of him in that context, was she? It was ridiculous. Even if she were the type to take lovers James Cade would be the last man she'd choose. He was dangerous and she was sensible. She shook her head at herself and deliberately drew in a deep, deep breath.

She was her own mistress and was a respected, highly paid employee with one of the country's most prestigious firms of tax specialists. And as soon as Petra was earning and able to support herself and the boys she, Zoe, would be able to afford to move into a place of her own and concentrate on pushing herself further and further up the ladder in her chosen career.

And the recent run-in with James Cade was simply an unfortunate blip and very soon now her life would settle down again and become satisfyingly predictable, smooth and secure. And, although she wasn't looking forward to spending time with that dreadful, unsettling man, she would sensibly view the exercise as insurance.

Her father would tell the truth. And Petra should be home by now and would back him up. And produce the twins' birth certificates. Not even James Cade could argue with that.

She was feeling better by the minute, even managed to put in some good work, and she was able to force her mind into a numbing blankness as she fought her way back to Peckham Rye by public transport.

But by the time she walked up the area steps that led from the basement to the street the roiling, bubbling feeling deep inside her was back to being a nuisance again. It shook her badly. She'd been so sure she could handle being in his company for the drive out to the Kent borders. The drive back would be easier because by then he wouldn't be able to stop apologising.

Just concentrate on that drive back, she instructed herself, sternly blanketing out the niggling thought that she should have worn something more sedate, something a little more sophisticated than a pair of old cut-offs that showed a great deal of naked leg and a well-washed T-shirt that had a definite tendency to cling.

But at least she had had the foresight to keep her hair pinned severely back. 'Foresight'? What was she thinking about? James Cade couldn't care less what she looked like, dammit! Her personal integrity was all he was interested in. Hadn't he so cuttingly remarked that he had no inclination, no desire to take her to bed and that, if the day ever dawned when he wanted to, he'd get her there—no trouble at all. Leaving her in no doubt that he wasn't remotely interested, that he'd find making love to her marginally more boring than scratching his left ankle.

Which was the way she wanted it. Precisely the way she wanted it. It made them quits, didn't it? she snarled at herself inside her head as she shifted uneasily from one canvas-shod foot to the other, peering down the street.

No sign of him. Just a billowy black lady sitting on the steps of one of the tall, dilapidated houses on the opposite side of the street, sunning herself on this warm June evening, calling out to a group of kids who were kicking a tin can around.

The purring, almost silent arrival of the sleek black car took her by surprise and she pivoted round, cursing the circumstances that made her blush like a juvenile and decided that the only way she could handle this was to pretend complete indifference.

He leaned over to open the passenger door and she got in without an acknowledgment, settled herself neatly and vowed that the only words to pass her lips would be the necessary directions to the cottage. They could have nothing worthwhile to say to each other until Dad and Petra had convinced him that she had more moral integrity than most.

And when he apologised, as he would have to, she would be magnanimous about it and then put the whole episode right out of her mind and get on with the rest of her life. But she wasn't so sure she'd be able to resist getting her own back and making more than a few scathing comments when he drawled damningly, 'Thanks for the leg-show.' Strangely sleepy-looking grey eyes drifted insultingly over her body, the slender length of her shapely legs irredeemably displayed by the shorts she'd unthinkingly, out of habit, chosen to wear. 'But I thought I'd made it clear I prefer to make the running. If I want to take up what's on offer I'll let you know. In the meantime, don't hold your breath.'

'You creep!' Zoe exploded, her newly found capacity for violent rage shocking her. She would have left the car but he had already drawn away from the kerb, accelerating smoothly. She would make him eat dirt, never mind humble pie, just see if she wouldn't!

'Don't let your natural arrogance mislead you. I'm offering nothing, Mr Cade.' The venom was nicely iced over now, much more controlled. 'Except the opportunity to meet my people and get some of the kinks in your brain straightened out. And I'm sorry if the way I'm dressed offends you. I simply didn't think. It's hot and I usually dress this way when I've nothing important to do in my spare time.'

Which should have put him in his place, but didn't because he said quellingly, 'That's not quite how you've encouraged me to read the situation. You invited, remember? I declined.' Then asked for directions as they reached a busy intersection, all in the same breath, and Zoe sat back in her seat and gave up because she was no masochist and saw no sense in beating her head against the brick wall of his firmly embedded, bigoted misconceptions.

She wasn't going to make an issue of it and lose her temper all over again. Time would tell, she told herself darkly and spoke only when spoken to, and that was merely to give directions.

It was eight when they finally parked outside the cottage. And, although she would miss the opportunity of seeing the twins, they did tend to make adult, sober conversation impossible and they would be safely tucked up in bed by now. But they weren't, because as she left

the car and waited for James Cade to join her by the
wicket gate she could hear them running around and
squealing.

Zoe's heart lifted a little because seeing the small boys
in the middle of the week was a bonus, then fell again
because Cade's presence at her side was dampening, to
say the least. And before they'd progressed halfway along
the path to the front door her father appeared in his
shirt sleeves, the expression of pleased surprise on his
face too genuine for even the mega-suspicious Cade to
doubt.

She had wondered whether to phone through and let
Dad know to expect them and was thankful now that
her instincts had led her to veto the idea. If their visit
had been expected then Cade would jump to the conclusion that she'd primed her family, told them what lies
to tell. Hadn't he previously said that was exactly what
he would expect her to do in these circumstances?

Horribly conscious of Cade, of the supple length of
his body clad in an understatement of casual, expensive
elegance, Zoe found it impossible to relax even in the
warmth of her father's affectionate hug. And tension
stuck her tongue to the roof of her mouth so it was left
to Cade to make the introductions, which he did with a
minimum of fuss, with none of the horrible accusations
which would explain his presence here.

'James Cade—your daughter and I are business colleagues.' The outstretched hand was clasped warmly and
Zoe tried to swallow the lump in her throat. Dad was
too straightforward to recognise a devious louse when
he saw one; he would throw a blue fit if he knew how
the younger man had maligned one of his precious
daughters. 'And you must be Zoe's sister.' Cade
glanced up.

Petra had appeared in the open doorway, a twin under each arm. Although her hair was a darker, richer blonde than Zoe's, her eyes blue rather than green, the family likeness was unmistakable. And she seemed completely unfazed by that piercing, level grey stare because her smile was bright and welcoming and she obviously couldn't see the wheels turning inside that clever, analytical brain.

'Sorry about the chaos.' Petra smiled wryly as each twin tried to wriggle free in energetic unison. 'But I didn't arrive home until this afternoon and these two little demons have got wildly over-excited.'

'Well, now.' Bill Kilgerran's arm was draped lightly around Zoe's shoulder, his affable smile for the younger man. 'Are you two just passing or can you stay for supper? It got held up because the two who should be seen but not heard were too hyped up to go to bed.'

'I'll give them their bath.' Zoe scooped up the tiny boys and carried them into the house, suddenly not caring what interpretation Wright and Grantham's chief executive put on the way she'd stepped in and taken over.

He could go right ahead and attribute it to maternal frustration with a liberal dosing of guilt if it pleased him to do so—and it most probably would. She, she decided, cuddling the two soft little bodies close, had had as much as she could take. Let James His Piousness Cade accept or decline the supper invitation as he thought fit, she was past caring what he did. Besides, her absence would mean he could start the inquisition into her character—or complete lack of same—without her having to sit by and squirm.

'I'll be up in twenty minutes with their warm milk,' Petra called from the foot of the stairs. 'Do the stern aunt act and you might get a result.'

Barely sparing a glance for James, who was looking at her as if she'd suddenly sprouted two heads, Zoe carried on up. Stern was something she was incapable of being with these two little charmers and bathtime, as she'd known it would, degenerated into a watery mayhem, leaving her soaked and breathless but mercifully free of anxiety because she'd left that downstairs with the relentlessly suspicious Cade. She wasn't even going to wonder how far the inquisition had progressed because if he'd started accusing her of using immoral earnings to supplement her salary, sleeping with so many men that she had no idea of who the twins' father was, itching to get her hands on his company's secrets so she could sell them to the highest bidder, then her father's roar of outrage would have brought the roof down.

And it was half an hour later when Petra poked her head round the bathroom door.

'I left their milk in the bedroom. How are you doing?'

'Fine,' Zoe puffed, rubbing baby powder on to two warm dry bodies. Two pairs of eyes were beginning to droop.

Petra nodded, stooping to help with the business of pyjamas, her voice low but obviously deeply impressed as she imparted, 'That man of yours is a knockout. Where did you find him? I'd ask for directions, only— but that's for later; I've so much to tell you!' She stood up, scooping Rickie into her arms while Zoe took Robin who was nearly asleep on his feet. 'So tell me, where did you meet him and how long has this been going on?'

'He's a business colleague.' Zoe's tongue fumbled over the words then she added repressively, 'Nothing's going on. And he's not my man, so you can get that idea right out of your head.'

'Oh, no? Pull the other one—it's got bells on it! You've never brought a man home before to meet the family—think I'm stupid?'

Yes, Zoe affirmed inside her head as she followed her sister out of the bathroom. Anyone who could think that she would ever be remotely attracted to a man as cold, as unfeeling, as mean-minded and downright arrogant as that bastard Cade just had to be stupid! If not downright insane.

But now wasn't the time to go into all that. There were things she had to know, but she bided her time until the boys had finished their milk and were tucked up. They had recently graduated to single beds and the three of them—theirs and Petra's—took up most of the floor space. Zoe knew her sister had dreams of saving hard and having an extension built on to the cottage—an extra, much needed bedroom and another living-room downstairs.

'Well, what's he been saying?' she demanded in a whisper. Robin was already firmly asleep and Rickie on the border.

'What should he be saying?' Petra arched one fine brow. 'Just talking. Dad's certainly taken to him—well, he's so easy to get on with, but you should know that.' She gave a tiny, cat-like conspiratorial smile that made Zoe want to groan aloud. 'You certainly picked a charmer, you old dark horse. He's so interested in everything—the boys, my new job, and when I told him about the Open University course he was most impressed!' She put an arm round Zoe's tiny waist and gave an affectionate squeeze. 'So I did the sisterly thing and confessed I couldn't have done it without your financial and moral support, and Dad's practical help, of course—I couldn't leave him out of the happy back-patting session, could I?'

Zoe smiled wanly. She might have guessed Cade wouldn't hurl accusations and questions around like a sledge-hammer; he had far too much style for that. He had simply, as Petra had put it, used his charm—which she, Zoe, had yet to see any evidence of—and allowed her unsuspecting family to answer the questions he hadn't asked.

She knew he was clever and she knew he could be cruel. She hadn't guessed he could be devious and charming at one and the same time, too. She shivered suddenly and Petra said, 'You're soaked. Despite your brains, when you and the twins get together you don't act much older than they are! Want to change into something of mine?'

'No.' Zoe shook her head. Getting soaked was all her own fault and her shorts and top would soon dry out. She wanted out, wanted to be on her own again, back in her basement room—and never mind if Jenna was entertaining her Henry right next door or, upstairs in the main part of the house, Gary and Hannah were enjoying their privacy. Which, unaccountably, made her feel lonely and a little bit lost, but she still needed to get away because she wouldn't be rid of Cade until he'd driven her back and dropped her off. And because she didn't want to ask a direct question she went the long way round—which wasn't like her at all—and said, 'I'll walk around outside to dry off while you finish making supper. That's if we're staying.'

'Of course you are. James said he'd be delighted.'

Which hadn't been what she'd wanted to hear at all. James might be delighted to prolong the agony but she wasn't. Although she should have been feeling blithely relieved, because by now he knew she'd been telling the truth, she wasn't. And she knew why when she followed Petra into the kitchen, hoping to sneak out into the garden by the back door, and found her father and James Cade already there.

Her father was stirring a rich, aromatic sauce and Cade, who had shed his lightweight jacket to reveal a black silk shirt tucked into fawn chinos, was feeding pasta into boiling water.

She would never have imagined him in a domestic role, not in a million years, and the way he turned and watched her was totally unnerving, making her staggeringly conscious of the length of leg she was displaying, the soaked T-shirt that clung wetly to her breasts, revealing every rounded curve, the deep indentation between.

That was why she instinctively knew she had to hide from him—the way he only had to look at her to make her conscious of her own body in a way she had never been before, and the way he could make something move deep inside her.

'What did you do—jump in the bath with them?' Bill Kilgerran asked, his grin splitting his face. 'My eldest's got a split personality, James—as you'll find out. Point her at your fixed assets and stock levels and she'll operate like a human computer; leave her alone with the twins for ten minutes and she can get even sillier and wilder than they are.'

Which made her the uneasy recipient of one of James Cade's humourless smiles and the piercing, steel-like spearing glint of those hooded grey eyes. And made her, for the first time ever, want to smack her father for drawing attention to her bedraggled state and her sometimes less than cool and sensible personality.

Wild and silly, indeed! Now that would be something he could feed all his doubts on, wouldn't it just! But she only ever got like that with her small nephews. She enjoyed playing with them, and spoiling them, too, probably because she'd missed out on so much in her own childhood. But Cade wouldn't see it that way. He'd see her alleged 'wildness' in quite a different context.

She didn't suppose he'd ever done anything silly in the whole of his life, ever felt any real emotion. He probably wasn't even human!

Not able to trust herself to make any comment at all, she swept through the kitchen and out of the back door unaware, as she'd always been, of her unconsciously provocative wiggle, but painfully aware of the way Cade watched every step of her progress because of the rash of goose-bumps all over her body, the tingle all the way down her spine.

And was only able to relax when she was alone, out in the long rambling garden, caressed by the warm evening air, the familiar feel of grainy, warm wood beneath her bare arms as she leant on the fence at the far end of the orchard and watched the cows browsing in the field beyond. Until, long, uncounted, contented minutes later, that dark fascinating voice said from right behind her,

'I've been sent to find you. Supper's ready.'

Drowsy relaxation was shot to pieces like the sudden bursting of a dreamily floating soap bubble, stiff-spined outrage taking its place as she straightened up, turned, her green eyes flashing storm warnings. His coolly leashed vitality coupled with all that arrogant, repressive self-confidence always made her feel angry and confused, not fully in control of herself and her life.

But it shouldn't. Not now, she informed herself quickly, consciously easing the tension out of her shoulders, allowing her eyelids to drift slowly down while she silently counted to ten. No need to get her knickers in a twist—not when he had charmed the truth out of her family.

Get that fact on record and she had nothing to worry about. Supper and then home and the pleasant prospect of getting on with the rest of her nice, predictable, secure life.

So get it on record, she nudged herself not looking at him, but aiming a tight little smile somewhere in his general direction.

'Can I take it you're satisfied with my credentials, Mr Cade?' She was pleased with that, pleased with the way she began to lead the way back through the orchard, walking quite briskly but not scurrying because that would have told him she had something to fear from him. And she didn't, not a thing.

But her face went tight with the temper she hadn't known she'd possessed until he'd come into her life as he countered damningly, 'You can. At least, I've decided to give you the benefit of the doubt until, and unless, I have fresh evidence to the contrary.'

'How magnanimous of you!' She could hardly believe anyone could be so blind, so meanly suspicious. 'I'm sure your own mother would be weak with pride at your generosity of spirit—that's if you ever had a mother, which I'm increasingly beginning to doubt!'

Unappalled by her loss of temper, the insult she'd tossed at him with such relish, she swung round to face him. She was almost beginning to enjoy the loss of control he forced on her. It was new, a novel sensation because her dealings with people were always so precise.

But she was unprepared for the way his own eyes went black with anger, for the tight grip of iron-hard hands as they grasped her upper arms with the suddenness of a striking cobra, or for the blatant savagery in his voice as he told her harshly, 'Tread carefully, Miss Kilgerran. Don't forget I've the power to stop your career in its tracks—or derail it entirely. So watch that blistering tongue of yours—it doesn't sit easily with the cool and serene image you try so hard to project.'

His voice, his hands, both trapped her, threatened her. Not the words he actually said though they were chilling enough, but the sheer menacing power of the deep, harsh-velvet tones that were somehow far more sexually arousing than something lighter, more charming, specifically designed to please.

Sexually arousing? Was she going mad? Yet what else could explain the thrusting, spiralling wild-fire deep in the most intimate core of her being? The febrile concentration of a shattering sensation that weakened every other part of her, hurtling her towards the point of collapse?

And why, even as she felt the relaxation of the sudden, desperate tension in him, recognised it in the slow gentling of his eyes, in the way his grip loosened on her arms, making it possible, if she had the will, to brush his hands aside and walk away, could she only stand there, as if the dark magic of him bound her, and not against her will, either?

She shuddered and he watched her, his eyes shuttered, hiding anger now, or perhaps he'd already forgotten he'd felt it. His hands were moving over her skin now, hypnotically arousing, not meant to soothe or comfort, not at all.

He knew, she thought dazedly, just what he was doing. And so did she. Some deep atavistic instinct told her exactly what he was doing and the female seemed in dire danger of succumbing to the will of the male and she swallowed drily as a sharply sweet kick of desire assaulted her and watched him watch the tiny ripple of her long, slender throat and heard him say, as soft as silk, 'If you need further warning to keep a guard on your tongue, don't forget your other offer. I might just be tempted to take you up on it. It could be interesting and might even be rewarding—and not only in the object of proving your truthfulness, or otherwise.'

CHAPTER FIVE

ZOE snapped her briefcase shut and surveyed her cleared desk with quiet satisfaction. The decision for her to go out to Portugal had been taken quickly; she'd been lucky to get a flight at such short notice at this time of year.

She'd known, of course, that she would have to go to do the audit on site, and as the factory premises where Wright and Grantham produced the bulk of their output—quite separately from the research and development centres here in the UK—were in the eastern Algarve, the Portuguese trip had been assured.

She hadn't expected to go out so soon but Luke had told her, 'You'll be met at Faro airport and driven to the villa. It's owned by W. and G. as a base for visiting executives. The height of luxury, by all accounts. I could do with a slice of sybaritic lifestyle myself—Julie's booked us into a caravan in Wales for the annual holiday. She says the kids will love it—I know I won't!'

Zoe hadn't questioned the decision about the audit— she didn't mind whether she did it this month or next— but she spared a few pitying thoughts for Luke's wife. He was obviously not enamoured of the idea of spending two weeks in a caravan with his wife and young children and didn't seem to mind who knew it. So much for love and marriage and sharing!

But the Taylors' sterile relationship was none of her business and she had far better things to think about. Such as the way James Cade had decided not to demand

her removal from his firm's accounts, had departed her
life as abruptly as he'd entered it.

She hadn't been at all sure, at first, that he would stop
prying into her credentials. That supper with her father
and Petra had been an ordeal she was doing her best to
forget. She'd been too incensed by his latest, most horrible threat to eat more than a couple of mouthfuls and
she'd been incapable of speech, listening to the devious
louse charm her family, worming details of their life out
of them without them being aware he was doing it. And
while she'd been helping her sister clear away, Petra had
grinned.

'Love makes fools of us all. It's certainly ruined your
appetite!'

And Zoe's repressive frown had merely produced a
gale of giggles and, although Zoe was happy that her
sister seemed far more relaxed and carefree since securing
her job and taking the holiday she'd had to be dra-
gooned into agreeing to, she could do nothing but
condemn her wrong-mindedness where her own relationship with Cade was concerned. And she could
hardly come out with the truth because that would be
too embarrassing for words.

And the journey home had been awful, too. Neither
of them had spoken. He had seemed deep in a brooding,
enigmatic silence which she, in her wisdom, had deemed
it best not broken. She couldn't trust her tongue when
he was around and with that stinging threat so fresh in
her mind—to watch what she said, or else—then staying
dumb was obviously the best policy.

Not that his odious and disgusting threat would ever
be carried out. She would rather hand in her notice and
support herself by selling matches on street corners than
go to bed with him!

Her face turned a violent, uncomfortable shade of red and she put her pale fingers up to her burning cheeks and made a soft sound of distress. Even thinking about him in that context set up a chain reaction inside her that was terrifying. She had to be going crazy! Because he hadn't meant it, of course he hadn't. It had been fury speaking, that was all. And now, looking back, she couldn't properly remember what she'd said to draw out all that blistering rage. Something to do with his mother...

Oh, grow up, do! she growled disgustedly at herself. It was over. Nothing further had been said about having her removed from his firm's accounts and he had not even turned up at that first formal meeting to impale her with those steely, assessing grey eyes.

So everything was fine. Just fine. She had briefed her secretary and her PA, satisfied herself that everything was sliding along on nicely oiled rails and had the trip to the Algarve to look forward to.

Determined to think positively, to relegate Cade, his accusations, his threats and the dreadful effect he had on her right to the very back of her mind from where, eventually, all those regrettable events would slip permanently out, she battled her way home.

If the villa was as luxurious as Luke had implied then she could look on the coming couple of weeks as a working holiday. No harm in that. She would do the job with all the speed and efficiency she was capable of and still have time to relax in the sun and enjoy herself.

When she eventually let herself into her basement flat she was feeling much more relaxed. There was no sign of Jenna so she had to be out and that was a bonus—privacy had been at a premium ever since they had had to share. And the first thing she did after changing into a scuffed pair of jeans and a warm sweatshirt, because the mini heatwave was well and truly over, was phone home.

She hadn't been to the cottage as usual last weekend because she'd needed the time to sort out her new quarters and she wouldn't be going this weekend, either, because she'd be in Portugal and she was itching to know how Petra's first few days as a working mum had gone.

'Fantastic!' Petra enthused down the line. 'Everything's working out beautifully. And Mrs Evans from down the road is turning out to be a treasure—she comes in a couple of hours each day, does some tidying round and keeps an eye on the boys to let Dad have some time to himself to recharge his batteries. And she charges next to nothing. She says she's only too happy to have something to occupy her time. Since her husband died a couple of years ago she hasn't known what to do with herself. And guess what——' her voice lowered conspiratorially '—she and Dad get on like nobody's business. He's taking her out tonight, to some swish restaurant or other. He's a bit closed-up about it and says he thinks she needs a bonus for her "tireless work and good humour" and got all miffed when I teased him about a romance! What do you think?'

'Lay off the teasing and keep your fingers crossed,' Zoe advised, a smile in her voice. She'd seen Barbara Evans often since she lived only a few hundred yards away from the cottage. She was pretty and plump and in her early fifties, with kind eyes and a ready smile. She and her husband hadn't been in the area for much longer than three months when he'd died of a sudden heart attack. When they'd discussed employing someone to come in for an hour or two, to give Dad a break when Petra began working at the agency, Barbara Evans had sprung immediately to mind. And it would be a big weight off her and Petra's minds if he could find a loving companion, someone he could allow to take their mother's place in his life. But it was very early days and Petra was burbling on.

'So it must be catching—romance in the air for all the Kilgerrans. Dad and Mrs E.—she asked me to call her Barbara, by the way—you and James...'

'And?' Zoe asked quickly into the sudden and uncharacteristic silence. She was going to ignore that bit about her and James. Petra wouldn't be convinced, no matter how hard she argued the opposite, and she really didn't want to have to think about him, much less talk about him. 'You mentioned all three of us?'

'Well...' Petra began soberly. 'I did meet someone on that holiday. Phil. He's a vet, recently qualified and a very junior partner with a practice near Leatherhead. His looks aren't in the same class as your James's, but I like him. A lot, actually. He's warm and straightforward and sensible and he didn't turn a hair when I explained about the twins. And before you say anything, I won't make the same mistake twice. Easy does it this time. I'll see how things work out.' Then, more brightly, her india-rubber character shining through, 'You'll meet him this weekend. He's coming to spend the day on Sunday. He said he'd arrive early so you'll have to be up and out of the sofa-bed in the sitting-room so as to have the place looking less like a pigsty when he shows up, and——'

'I won't be there,' Zoe cut in quickly, and explained about the business trip, said her goodbyes and told herself to stop feeling lonely.

It would be wonderful if Dad and Petra both found love, a caring partner to share their separate futures with.

She, Zoe, couldn't hope for anything more for them, and she was only feeling a bit desolate and out of it because the three of them had been so close, so interdependent, for so long now.

Zoe shook her head, impatient with herself. She didn't really need anyone, did she? She was an independent lady, successful in her career and going places—like Portugal, tomorrow, for instance—and all these senseless internal mutterings weren't getting her packing done.

The Wright and Grantham factory was on the outskirts of Loule. Zoe plucked the notes she'd made out of her handbag. The paper was beginning to look battered round the edges because she'd consulted it often on the flight to Faro, though it didn't tell her any more now than it had done on all those other occasions.

But it was something to do because the man who had met her at the airport, holding up a placard with her name on it, obviously spoke no English and looked like a gangster. He had carried her luggage to the waiting car, a long black Mercedes with tinted windows, ushering her pointedly into the back seat.

Her conversational gambits had been met with silence and Zoe had pushed her Portuguese phrase book back into her bag and decided that it must be her atrocious pronunciation at fault rather than a surly arrogance on his part. At least she hoped so because, presumably, he would be driving her to the factory each day and back to the villa in the evening.

The Villa Rosa was, according to what Luke had told her, roughly six miles from Loule, not far from São Bras, and they had left the attractive town behind them several minutes ago and were driving through orange groves into rugged open countryside where everything shimmered in a haze of midsummer heat.

Thankful for the air-conditioning, Zoe leant back against the soft leather upholstery and refused to worry about the silent treatment she was getting from the driver. After her recent run-ins with James Cade—outcome entirely successful—she would never worry about anything else again! A couple of weeks here, doing the job she was paid well to do, seeing as much of the area as she could, and then back to London, the office, losing herself in her work and, in her spare time, looking for a decent place to live.

So everything was looking good now and she was still basking in a glow of serene optimism when the car swung between gateposts, down through an avenue of cypress trees and came to a halt in front of a sprawling, white-painted, beautifully maintained villa.

Not waiting for the driver to open her door, Zoe got out, blinking as the heat and the white shimmering light hit her senses and was still trying to get acclimatised to the sheer exoticism of it all as a slight young woman, neat in severe black, yet with a wickedness sparkling in dark, dark eyes and a lushly curved mouth which defied the strictures of her uniform, glided over the paving slabs and said, 'Miss Kilgerran? I am Isabel. Isabel Silva. I am to look after you while you are here.' She held out a small, capable-looking hand and Zoe shook it enthusiastically, glad the other girl—housekeeper?—spoke English, with such an appealing accent, too, and was as unlike the taciturn driver as it was possible to get. 'James has given detailed instructions. First, you will want to shower and rest after your journey. Come, I will show you.'

She turned her smile on the driver who was extracting the luggage from the boot and Zoe thought frantically, What's James Cade got to do with anything? Then calmed herself down with the mental reminder that his company owned this place and he would, without doubt, have told the staff to expect the accountant from England and issued instructions accordingly.

'Vitor will take your things to your room.' A slight touch on Zoe's arm turned her thoughts from the man whose existence she would prefer to forget. 'Vitor needs to be explained—to those who do not know him. First, he is my big brother and loved by all who do know him— that is the most important. Second, he is a deaf mute since birth. It was difficult for him, especially as he is an intelligent man. Always, the family tried to help but his pride was gone until James met him, and understood. He gave him work here—he drives for the company, helps with the villa grounds, and at the factory. If something breaks down, Vitor can fix it. He has a natural understanding of machines, even the most complex. And James took the time to learn signing, to communicate in our language, you understand? Senhor Cade is a truly wonderful man, don't you think?'

Zoe most definitely did not. But she wasn't about to say so and cause a whole heap of friction. After all, the Portuguese girl had good reason to be grateful. And as seeing Cade as a sensitive, caring altruist was a shock to her system, and not something she wanted to dwell on since she would prefer not to let him into her head at all, she didn't answer, and made admiring noises about the interior of the villa as Isabel led her along cool corridors to her room.

Luke hadn't been exaggerating when he'd spoken of luxury. The room she'd been given was like a vast underwater cave, decorated in toning greens and blues, the floor coolly tiled, long windows shadily louvred, enough mirrored hanging cupboards to satisfy the most dedicated follower of fashion and a huge double bed that looked infully comfortable.

Her luggage had already been delivered, plus a cooler-jug of freshly squeezed orange juice, and Isabel said, 'If you need anything more, you only have to ring. I'll serve dinner on the terrace at nine and if you feel in the mood there's a pool you can use.'

If she felt in the mood! Zoe bubbled to herself as she pottered happily around the en suite bathroom. The sunken bath, set in its marble surround, looked big enough to swim in, but the pool most definitely called, loud and clear. She could quite easily get used to this lifestyle, she decided, sparing a fleeting thought for her shared basement, the unpredictable British weather, the daily fight to get to work by public transport.

Here she would be chauffeur-driven, no less, and would have this beautiful, luxurious place to herself, no jostling for kitchen or bathroom space. Heaven!

Settling herself into her swimsuit, her reflection thrown back at her by at least a dozen full-length mirrors, she decided she looked almost indecent. But no amount of tugging and tweaking could make the black one-piece look less flaunty—cut shamefully high in the leg and low in the bosom, it made her look like a total stranger to herself.

Only once before had she looked at herself and cringed, and that had been when Jenna had dressed her up for that ill-fated Tarts and Vicars thrash. She hadn't been swimming since leaving school and she'd shopped for hot-weather holiday gear in a necessary hurry, not having time to try anything on, just going on sizes. She'd had no idea that the black Lycra one-piece would look so—so, well, sexy...

She was used to looking in character, like a sensible no-nonsense little tax specialist. She liked looking like a sensible, no-nonsense little tax specialist...

But the bubbly mood which had afflicted her ever since she had seen the Villa Rosa took over and she averted her eyes from the many embarrassing images the mirror threw back at her, took the pins out of her hair and braided it into a plait. There was no one around to comment or raise eyebrows. Except Isabel and Vitor, and they would be too well-trained to do anything so rude. Which reminded her—when she ran across Vitor again, now that she knew he wasn't being surly or plain bolshie, she would give him her biggest, warmest smile and not look sideways at him out of wary eyes as if he were some kind of thug!

So, dismissing the way she looked as totally irrelevant, she grabbed a tube of sun-block, a shady hat and dark glasses and trotted out.

The winding staircase took her down to the circular marble-paved hall. There were no doors, she discovered, in the main living area, simply graceful archways leading into sumptuous rooms and, through one of them, she saw open french windows, a balustraded terrace, an inviting glimpse of sparkling azure water.

Pulling in a deep, excited breath, Zoe swayed on through, resisting the impulse to run and hurl herself into the water and shriek with joy. But that would be childish and she was never childish—except when she was around the twins and that was different, something she was unable to help.

Pausing briefly on the terrace, she closed her eyes blissfully and revelled in sensation as the sun stroked all that exposed skin with its scorching caress. There was something very nearly pagan about such heat, something that made her want to strip off the scrap of black Lycra and, she realised with a jolt of surprise, she might have done just that if Isabel and Vitor weren't somewhere around. Then went into deep, deep shock as that never-to-be-forgotten voice—the dark harsh-velvet tones slicked over now with smooth courtesy—came out of the shimmering, hot scented air.

'Ah, Zoe. Has Isabel settled you comfortably? Did you have a good flight?' Then, an injection of husky amusement making a sham of social good manners, 'Had I realised how interesting the transition would be, I would have made the effort to meet you at the airport myself.'

Please God, it wasn't possible! The sudden violent lurch of her heart made her feel queasy and there was no doubting the evidence of her own eyes as she opened them warily and peered through fringing lashes at the man she had hoped never to have to meet face to face again. At least not yet, and not like this!

James Cade was stretched out on one of the padded poolside loungers and he rose with an indolent grace that reminded Zoe uncomfortably of a great stalking cat. One of the more deadly varieties. Wearing merely the bare essential in the way of boxer shorts, there was far too much honed, olive-toned masculine perfection on view, and Zoe spat out unthinkingly, defensively, 'What are you doing here?' Spoiling all this perfection, that was what he was doing. The serpent in the garden of Eden had nothing on him! 'Keeping an eye on me? Afraid I might set up a stall in Loule market and sell your company's secrets to anyone prepared to hand over a few escudos?' And felt the breath punch out of her lungs when he smiled.

It transformed his face, wiping out the austere severity, making her senses reel in breathless fascination. And the steel of his eyes turned to glittering diamonds of intimate amusement as he said, his voice a whispery slither that made her toes curl, 'Taking a short break. Even monsters need them from time to time. But keeping an eye on you would be no hardship at all.' And went on to prove it, his slowly roving glance like a lover's caress, touching, skimming, lingering.

Quickly, her breath thickening in her throat, her hands flew up to cover her breasts. Pouting, hardening, blatantly pushing against the sleek black Lycra—madness! She didn't know what was happening to her! Or rather, she did—she knew quite well because she wasn't that wet behind the ears. But she didn't know why!

Tossing her hat and sun-block on to the nearest lounger, she dived into the water before he could do any more damage to her self-esteem. Sadly out of practice, she swam one length with difficulty and no style whatsoever, and mourned her lack of control. Why he, of all the men she had ever come into contact with, should be able to draw such a blatant sexual response from her virginal body was something she couldn't understand. So, OK, he was a terrifyingly gorgeous male, but his nasty suspicious nature, all the grief and aggro he had given her, should completely negate the way he looked, shouldn't it?

And where had all her cherished pragmatism gone? Why couldn't she handle him and the utterly humiliating physical effect he had on her? She came up, blowing, at the far end, dashing the water out of her eyes to see two long, tanned, hair-roughened legs planted firmly on the pool surround, then felt the hard, no-

nonsense grip of his hands on her arms as he hauled her out.

Water sluiced off her, moulding the skimpy black Lycra even more indecently close to her body, and Zoe couldn't breathe. And that wasn't entirely due to her inept flailing activities in the pool, she recognised with reluctant honesty. Their two nearly naked bodies were much too close and the touch of his hands on her arms sent a series of sensations scudding through her, blowing her mind, weakening her bones, breaking through all those defensive barriers.

She wanted him to kiss her, hold her. Crazy, but true. She needed to feel that hard, honed body absorbing her soft, damp curves, mastering, sweeping away the frail barriers of her mind, and for one shattering moment as she saw the flicker of fire deep in those heavily lidded silver irises she thought it was going to happen and her eyes drifted shut as incandescent flames scorched through her bloodstream, her limpid body moving unconsciously closer to the heated magnetism of his in basic and mindless female surrender. But the cool mockery of his tone as his hands slid back to his sides devastated her utterly and she dipped her head in humiliation as his words washed over her.

'Why so defensive, Zoe? What made you so suddenly decide to go for a swim when you barely know the rudiments? A complete lack of manners, or a big guilty conscience?' The mockery deepened as he scooped a towel from a lounger and tossed it to her. 'You're not making a very good job of convincing me you've nothing to hide.'

Smothered in the fluffy folds of the towel she felt marginally better, more in control. She had acted thoughtlessly, she conceded, but wasn't about to confess that simply seeing him was enough to send her into a witless panic.

Something that was going to have to change.

Beginning now.

And he was walking back towards the terrace end of the pool and that made it easier although the brief boxer shorts wickedly emphasised the near nakedness of that superb body, the long, muscular legs, the sheer power of wide rangy shoulders that tapered to the narrow waist and lean, mean hips...

Oh, stop it! she snarled at herself, and made her feet patter after him, making a deliberate attempt to get her mind in order.

He had dropped on to one of the loungers, relaxing back in the shade of a solitary orange tree. Ignoring the temptation to scuttle back to her room, she sank down on a padded stool, the towel still clutched around her, and told him with a small dismissive smile, 'Forgive my lack of manners. My mind had been on next week. On work. I hadn't expected to see——' she had been about to say 'you' but amended quickly '—anyone here. You surprised me.' She hadn't been thinking of work at all but it wasn't lying, it was composure. And that was the name of the game, had to be, when dealing with James Cade. She forced herself to meet the vaguely withering assessment of those narrowed grey eyes. 'I have nothing to hide, as I believe you already know.'

'I wonder.' Black brows lifted. 'I find you something of an enigma.' He smiled without humour. 'I feel that nothing about you is quite what it seems.' He silenced the unguarded protest she was about to make with the slow movement of one hand. 'Humour me. Let's start with your reaction just now. If your fishwife comments and abrupt and unlovely immersion in the pool didn't hide a guilty conscience then what, I wonder, sparked it off?'

He was like a chess player, she thought, coldly horrified. He was looking for weak points in her defence, a way to get past her guard. He was clever enough to find it, too. Would he be amused, disgusted or just plain pitying if he ever found out that although her logical mind told her she loathed him her body said something else entirely? It blindly responded to him as if he were the one man fate had created expressly for her!

She would almost rather, she thought, getting hot and bothered beneath the swamping, smothering folds of the towel, prefer him to keep on thinking she had something reprehensible to hide, that her weird reaction to finding him here had been due to the guilty conscience he'd decided she had.

And was saved from having to find a response as a sulky female voice declared, 'Why didn't you wake me, James? You know I don't like sleeping too long in the afternoon. Who's that? Oh, that book-keeper woman, I suppose.'

Book-keeper woman! Despite the interruption, Zoe's eyes were firmly fixed on James's face, noting the flicker of irritation quickly suppressed by a lazy smile as he got slowly to his feet and made the introductions and Zoe's eyes popped wide open as she swivelled round.

So this was Stephanie Wright, the woman who was set to become James Cade's wife, if Luke was right about the rumours! Not even the obviously expensive designer culottes and toning waistcoat, the glossy make-up and artfully styled riot of long black hair could disguise the fact that his chairman's daughter was decidedly overweight and unredeemably plain.

And unpleasant with it, Zoe discovered as her out-stretched hand was ignored, the other woman's heavy features darkening with pique as she reminded him, 'We were going out, you promised—and you're not even dressed.'

'Easily remedied, Steph,' James pacified gently. 'You wouldn't want to leave before we'd seen our house-guest settled in.'

Which linked them firmly as a couple. Zoe knew his calming words had been meant to do just that and she didn't know why she should feel so wrathful. And as far as Stephanie Wright was concerned their house-guest could go boil her head, that much was obvious from the scornfully dismissive glance.

Zoe shot to her feet. Luke had been right, Stephanie was a first-class bitch—and not even remotely attractive—so he *was* considering marriage to his chairman's daughter merely to cement his career. As far as she was concerned, they deserved each other.

And, not really knowing why she did it, she allowed the smothering folds of the towel to fall away, pooling at her feet, displaying the immodest cut of the black Lycra number, gave James a sultry, teasing smile, simpered huskily, 'It was sweet of you to look after me, James. I enjoyed every minute. So run along and do as you're told—I'm quite capable of finding my own amusements, as I think you know.' And walked slowly back to the villa, conscious, for the first time ever, of the seductive sway of her svelte little body.

CHAPTER SIX

AND conscious of his eyes on her the whole time. Zoe actually felt them burning through her back as she met Vitor in the open french windows, going out to the terrace, and gave him her most brilliant smile because now she knew his silence didn't stem from surliness she deeply regretted all those wary looks she'd given him and wanted them to be friends.

Vitor blinked, then grinned right back, making a sweeping gesture for her to pass and she did, swaying her hips, and she couldn't be sure—not through the constant drone of Stephanie's complaining voice—but she thought she'd caught a grunt of masculine disapproval coming from the poolside.

Not that she cared. As long as James Cade found no fault with her work over the coming two weeks he could disapprove of her, personally, as much as he liked. And that would make them equal because she thought he was the pits—coldly planning to marry that awful woman simply because it would be a good career move!

Not that she cared about that, either, she told herself as she made her way back to her room. They were welcome to each other. They would spoil another couple. And she'd give him half an hour to change and escort his portly fiancée to wherever they were going—as stringently commanded—and then take herself on a tour of the grounds and enjoy the rest of her first day here, ending up with the solitary and peaceful dinner out on the terrace that Isabel had promised. Lovely!

Putting on fresh undies, she made an unhurried selection from the new things she'd bought for this trip. She'd never been abroad before—the way things had been she'd had other things to spend her money on— holidays had been a luxury she hadn't been able to afford—and she'd spent a little too wildly when she'd embarked on that frantically rushed shopping spree. But she didn't regret it, not for an instant, because her reflection assured her she looked quite different from her normal sedately prim self.

The dress she had chosen was fashioned from cool fine cotton, almost gauzy, the bloused bodice sleeveless and deeply scooped at the neckline, front and back, the narrow skirt finishing well above her knees and the dark navy colour, sprigged with tiny white spots, suiting her fair skin. It managed to make her look much more attractively feminine than her battleaxe grey suits and old jeans and tops had ever done.

Yes, and sexy, too, she decided as she twisted in front of one of the mirrors for a rear view and noted the way the fine fabric clipped her neat bottom. And didn't stop to wonder why that should make her feel elated—and strangely restless—but unbraided her damp hair and let it fan out around her shoulders.

It was still blisteringly hot so, skirting the now deserted poolside, she stepped down on to a broadly sweeping semi-circle of lush green lawn—no doubt kept in such beautiful condition by the ministrations of Vitor—and walked slowly towards the beckoning shade of a stand of pine trees beyond a lavish planting of pink oleanders and wine-red roses.

A strategically placed wooden seat, complete with invitingly soft scatter cushions, drew her. Suddenly, the day felt as if it had been going on for a very long time indeed, and she sank gratefully down among the cushions, relaxing, fanning herself with the guide book she'd brought along to help her plan off-duty treats for herself.

Although excursions around the immediate countryside no longer carried the tag of self-indulgences in her mind, they would be more like essential strategies if she were to spend as little time as possible at the Villa Rosa in the company of James Cade and his bucket-faced bride to be.

Oh, catty! she remarked to herself, opening the book and spreading the integral large-scale map of the area out on her knees. She was one of the least catty people she knew, normally, and Stephanie Wright couldn't help having a face like a bucket and, normally again, she would never have dreamed of commenting on the fact, not even within the privacy of her own thoughts; but she had taken an instinctive deep dislike to the other woman which was probably down to her dismissive rudeness, she decided complacently.

Or because of her relationship with James? The thought popped unbidden into her head, and she viewed it with no complacency at all and thrust it right out again and concentrated fiercely on the map, wondering which part of the coastline she should try to hit first, wondering whether she should hire a car at the first opportunity...

And woke with a painful crick in her neck and wondered if she was still dreaming because James was standing over her, as impossibly, dauntingly attractive as ever, all that masculine potency coming off him in swamping waves. Waves so real she knew that if she reached out her hand she would be able to touch them and would be sucked into the forcefield.

She blinked, her breath catching in her throat. He had walked through her dreams and was now watching her wakening, and it was more than inconsiderate of him— it was downright unfair. It made her feel totally vulnerable, open to him, scared he would be able to see a reflection of the shamingly explicit dreams she'd had of him deep in the green pools of her eyes.

'Isabel's about to serve dinner. She sent me to find you.'

His voice slid over her, a velvet curl of amusement which sent tiny shudders down her spine, and she struggled to get to her feet, the pain in her neck making her wince and his hands came out to help her, his voice warmly sympathetic as he announced, 'Stiff. What else would you expect? That bench wasn't designed for catnaps.' The hands that had cupped her elbows, steadying her, slid softly over the bare skin of her arms, drifting over her shoulders, pushing aside the tumbled mass of her loose blonde hair and finding the seat of the pain.

The effect of his touch was startling. Zoe's eyes widened, fixed on the grainy texture of his olive-toned skin where it covered the hard, slashing line of his cheekbones and knew, heaven help her, that she wanted to touch. Wanted to, quite desperately.

She made a helpless soft mewing sound in her throat and he said quietly, 'Relax. I'll iron the knots out for you.'

Helplessly, her head dropped forward, finding the haven of his broad chest as his lean fingers soothed and stroked the muscles at her nape. But there was danger in this haven, she acknowledged chokily. Infinite danger in the way her body melted, flowing into his, his warmth, his hard masculinity drawing her to him as inevitably as the moon tugged the tides.

In a way it was terrifying, this loss of will, this instinctive capitulation to the dark magic of this man. Just this man. She knew she should have hated the feeling of lack of control, but couldn't because although it scared her it excited her, too, flooding her with wild sensations she hadn't known existed until now.

Impulsively, her arms twined around his body as she felt her breasts peak, and she pressed herself against him because every inch of her quivering flesh needed to fuse with the hard maleness of his, and felt the sharply sweet shock-wave of desire flare to life deep inside her as the span of her hips met the heat of his.

And beneath her fingertips she felt the fluid muscles of his back go tense. And there was a moment of utter stillness, a heartbeat of silence when the world held its breath and, dismayed, disorientated, she felt him push her away and she tottered, swayed, her legs unsteady. This time he made no move to support her and his mouth was grim in a face of stone as he said with a chilling lack of inflection, 'Remember mealtimes in future. Isabel has better things to do than hang around waiting until you decide to show up.' And he walked away, his wide shoulders rigid beneath the crisp white shirt he wore above wickedly sexy narrow-fitting black jeans, and Zoe blinked, swallowing hard. And no, she wasn't near to tears; she was shocked, that was all.

Shocked by his unnecessary rudeness, that was all, she assured herself, following more slowly. She hadn't deliberately fallen asleep, forgetting the time. Shocked by her reaction to him, too, but she couldn't be blamed for that, or not entirely, she comforted herself as somehow she got her ragged breathing back under control and tried to ignore the ache of frustration inside her.

For some deeply incomprehensible reason she'd been dreaming of him, and he'd woken her and she hadn't quite known where she was. She'd been muzzy and disorientated, still half asleep when he'd pulled her to him and massaged the muscles of her cricked neck. So, what she had felt had been pure fantasy, not real at all, an out-of-the-world continuation of the dream she'd been having.

Only thinking of that dream, of what had been happening, made her face flare up with heat. So she pushed it right out of her mind and concentrated on the wretched prospect of sharing what had been the promise of a pleasant, solitary, leisurely meal with that pompous creep and the unpleasant female he was planning to marry because of who her father was.

Having successfully translated all that regrettable sexual energy into righteous anger, she was firing on all cylinders, ready to wish the couple a blistering goodnight and sweep supperless to bed, thus letting them know she would rather starve than share a table with them, endure Stephanie's gibes about book-keepers and the unpredictability that was par for the course from James. And had the wind taken out of her sails when she saw the table on the terrace, two covers only, and James waiting with cool politeness to hold out a chair for her.

The patio light shed a soft gleam over silver and crystal, a variety of cold dishes, a bottle of *vinho verde*. Zoe hesitated and the opportunity to sweep away, using the blistering comment she'd been rehearsing over the last dozen or so paces, was lost. She sat, eyeing him warily as he took his own seat opposite, and blurted out, 'From your nasty remarks about mealtimes I imagined I was holding everything up—Isabel patiently keeping food hot, and all that. Do you enjoy making people feel guilty? People in general, or only me?'

His face darkened and she knew she was playing with fire. He wouldn't be used to being spoken to that way, by anyone—let alone mere underlings. Normally she was the most diplomatic soul alive, especially where her job was concerned, because it was too important to her to put at risk. She didn't know what had come over her, what had prompted her into taking this confrontational stance, and would have liked to have called the words back, and wished she could.

All he said was, 'Do you object to a cold supper? If so, I could ask Isabel to fix you something hot.'

'No, not at all.' Zoe kept her eyes on the plate in front of her. It was white with a prettily scalloped gold-leaf rim. She couldn't look at him because she was belatedly wondering if he had noticed the way she'd clung to him, wriggled against him as if she couldn't get close enough, almost begging him to make love to her. The embarrassment was dreadful. And her voice came out breathily as she added lamely, 'It all looks lovely.'

'Then help yourself. Don't feel you have to stand on ceremony.'

He sounded quite normal so perhaps luck was with her and he hadn't noticed that aberration of hers down under the pines.

She hoped so, she most certainly hoped so, because she had been acting completely out of character and she'd rather enter her coffin as a dried up old spinster than let him anywhere near her in a sexual context because, undeniably attractive though he was, she didn't like him. In fact, she rather thought she loathed him.

Which was a comfort, and allowed her to load her plate with a selection from the delicious cold meats, tiny rolls, succulent salads and cheeses on offer, and when he filled their glasses with the slightly sparkling white wine she was confident enough to remark, 'I thought you and Miss Wright were going out.'

'I changed my mind. She didn't.'

Interesting. Zoe regarded him with her head tilted on one side. So he didn't always dance to Stephanie's commanding tune. Looking at him, the hard planes of his face thrown into relief by the overhead lamplight, he didn't look like a man who would do a single damn thing he didn't want to do. Which meant that he hadn't accompanied his future wife to wherever it was they had planned to go because he had decided he couldn't be bothered.

Did Stephanie understand? Did she know she would be tying herself to a man who didn't love her? To a man who couldn't be bothered to try to please her, who wouldn't do a single thing for her if there wasn't something in it for him?

Suddenly, she began to feel sorry for the other woman. If she was in love with James but knew he had only proposed because of who her father was she must be feeling desperately miserable, knowing that falling in love wasn't an automatic passport to happiness. And maybe, earlier, they'd been quarrelling because she wanted to go out and he couldn't be bothered. Which might account for the surly, dismissive reception she'd given her.

It was certainly something to consider and Zoe, busily assuaging her healthy appetite, decided to give Stephanie Wright the benefit of the doubt. Even though she was only going to be here for a couple of weeks, with most of that time spent at the factory, the two of them might become friends. It took a lot of mental agility to imagine that happening, but Zoe was determined now to give it a try so she asked, 'How long will you and your intended be on holiday here?' and watched his face go blank, his fork freeze in mid-air.

What had she said wrong now? Was he so all-fired arrogant that he thought such a personal question—even one so innocuous—to be a gross impertinence, coming from her?

'My what?' he bit out, his brows knotting together in a frowning black bar, and Zoe shrugged slightly, refusing to be intimidated, laid down her fork and picked up her wine glass.

The pompous prig was probably deeply affronted that a creature like her had dared to mention his bride-to-be with her sullied breath.

She would never forget the vile things he'd said and thought of her, and never forgive that parsimonious 'I've decided to give you the benefit of the doubt until, and unless, I have fresh evidence to the contrary' which had been the nearest he'd been able to get to an apology.

And he might be impossibly attractive, at the top of his chosen career, probably rotten rich and, temporarily at least, her boss—but he wasn't God, and she wasn't going to treat him as if he were. So she said slowly and clearly, as if she were talking to an idiot, 'Your intended bride. Your fiancée. The woman you are going to marry. Stephanie Wright, remember?'

'And where did you hear that?' The voice was silky smooth, the frown had vanished, leaving his impressive features without expression. It was quite dark now and the lamplight bound them in a small world of their own. Zoe didn't feel comfortable with that feeling and shifted uneasily in her seat.

'I heard a rumour; apparently there'd been something in the papers.' She wasn't going to drop Luke in it; she was too loyal for that.

She drained her glass, reflecting that it might be sensible if she took her obviously contentious presence off to her own room, but he refilled her glass and didn't comment on her reply, and she might have been mistaken but she was sure she saw a look of relief deep in those unfathomable dark eyes just before he commented, 'Time to talk shop, I think. I'll drive you into Loulé in the morning and introduce you to Ben Bishop, the factory manager. He's English, so you won't run into language problems and his secretary speaks a smattering, too, so that should help. They'll make all you need available. Vitor will pick you up at five-thirty and ferry you back and forth from then on. Oh, and there's a good works canteen so you won't have to waste time looking for somewhere to eat at lunchtime.'

Fine, but she might prefer to explore the town a little during her lunch-break. She didn't bother to mention it but said instead, 'I'd like to see something of the area while I'm here—out of working hours, of course. How do I go about hiring a car?'

'No need.' He leaned back in his chair and his voice was warmly expansive as he told her, 'Vitor's at your disposal at all times. Just tell me or Isabel where you want to go and when, and we'll make sure he understands your wishes.' Reminding her that he had taken the trouble to learn sign language, given Vitor satisfying work, given him his self-respect.

The knowledge didn't sit easily with her conceptions of him, with the way he had treated her—only very tiny flashes of normal human consideration showing through the otherwise consistent distrust and dislike. The few sexual remarks she chose to ignore, not taking them into her calculations because they hadn't been meant—or only as a put-down.

And into her small, uncomfortable silence he began to talk, asking her about her work, why she had chosen such a specialised career, about her background, and somehow the conversation veered on to personal likes and dislikes and, strangely, she discovered they had a lot in common, and talking to him came so easily that she didn't realise Isabel had brought coffee out to them until she found a steaming cup in front of her.

She was seeing the charm Petra had spoken about, and didn't trust it because she didn't trust herself. She didn't want to like him. She wanted to hate him because she felt safer that way, and reminded herself of the way he'd threatened her job, regarding her as a security risk because he'd decided she slept around, giving sexual favours in return for cash or other favours.

But that didn't work, either. For the first time she could see his side of the story. All the circumstantial evidence had been against her, and no man who took his heavy responsibilities as seriously as he did could have afforded to ignore it. And at least he had told her of his misgivings, his doubts about her integrity and the possible consequences of it to her face. He had given her fair warning of his intention to demand her removal. He didn't stab people in the back.

She drank her coffee and sighed. She really ought to make a move, excuse herself and go to bed. But the evening, on the whole, had turned out better than she'd expected, given its impossible beginning, and the air was soft and warm now, the blistering heat of the day dissipated, the slight breeze carrying the seductive scent of orange blossom from the groves beyond the villa's grounds, and James was an excellent companion when he chose to be...

He asked, 'How's Petra getting along in her job? Have you heard? And what about Bill—how is he coping with the twins on his own?'

And because he'd bothered to remember, because he sounded interested, she gave him her wide, dazzling smile and found herself telling him everything, even down to Petra's hopes of a romance between her father and Barbara Evans, and ended up, 'It would be wonderful if he could find someone. Mum's death devastated him. He never stopped mourning her so it would be nice if he was over that at last, he's the sort who needs a close and permanent companion in his life. And he sacrificed so much for Petra and me. But what about your family, James?' His name slipped easily from her tongue. 'Are both your parents still alive? Do you have any brothers or sisters?'

Knowing more about him, his family and background, would flesh him out, make him seem closer somehow, and she didn't stop to wonder why that should seem so important now, only caught her breath in aching sympathy when he came back quickly with a coldly emphatic, 'No.'

Even then reality didn't impinge. His harsh negative had touched her heart, right where it hurt. Family was all-important to her, the bonds deep and all-embracing. She couldn't imagine what she would feel like if Dad, Petra and the twins weren't around.

'I'm sorry.' She reached out impulsively to touch his hand. It must be dreadful to have no one close, no one to share long childhood memories with, triumphs or disasters—large or small—only fully understood by those with close blood ties. And felt the warm flesh and bone beneath her sympathetic hand go very still. Until he dragged his hand from hers as if her skin were contaminated.

His voice was spiked with frost as he stood up from the table and told her, 'I don't like prying women, remember that. Keep your instincts to gossip to yourself in future.'

Gossip? Zoe stared at him blankly for a long pole-axed moment. He looked impressively intimidating. A shudder inched its way painfully down her spine. He'd asked her enough about her life, her family. That hadn't been gossiping or prying, oh, no, of course not! One rule for the high and mighty James Cade, another one entirely for a mere underling!

She felt hurt, callously dismissed, all her impulsive sympathy coldly rejected. But she wouldn't let herself be hurt. She wasn't that stupid.

Staring into the impatient, cruel face, she decided he was probably still sore about the news of his engagement to Stephanie getting out. The more people who knew about it—people like Luke Taylor, for instance—the more his reasons for marrying someone as physically unattractive and bitchy as his chairman's daughter would be sniggered about.

He wouldn't want to be a laughing stock.

Zoe shot to her feet, too, not looking at him now because she couldn't bear the thought of him making love to that woman. To any woman. The unstoppable mind pictures were intolerable.

Not stopping to work out her motivations, she said very tartly, 'I'll say goodnight, Mr. Cade. I'm sure your fiancée will be back soon. You'll both be eager to get to bed.'

That should cut him down to size, rub his nose in his reasons for proposing marriage to his chairman's daughter!

But he didn't sound in the least way diminished as he came back suavely, 'Your claws are showing, Zoe. You couldn't be jealous, could you?'

CHAPTER SEVEN

JEALOUS! That taunt still pricked her on the raw, coming back to haunt her, to bring the colour flying to her cheeks at completely unexpected moments during the day, even though she believed her mind was fully concentrated on her work.

Jealous? She wouldn't be in Stephanie's shoes if someone paid her in sacks of diamonds!

All last night's sympathy for the other woman had vanished completely this morning. Zoe had had to force herself to appear at a respectable time for breakfast, bearing in mind James had told her he would be driving her into Loule.

Aggravatingly, she'd overslept—which wasn't surprising considering the difficulty she'd had in calming her mind down sufficiently to find the oblivion her tired body craved—and hadn't had time to secure her hair in its no-nonsense knot, had had to leave it loose, clipped back from her face with a couple of pins. Otherwise, her appearance had been quite respectable, her white shirt-blouse teaming soberly with one of her grey suit skirts and sensible flat-heeled shoes.

Satisfied that the way she looked gave no indication of the churned-up sensations that were wreaking havoc inside her, she found the other two taking an al fresco breakfast at the poolside. James, casually dressed in black jeans and stone-coloured T-shirt, was urbanity itself, pulling up a chair for her, insisting she take more than the glass of freshly squeezed orange juice which was all she had felt she could stomach.

Forcing down a toasted roll, Zoe, remembering her decision of the evening before, had done her best to offer Stephanie a few friendly overtures. But the other woman had pointedly ignored her, just briefly raising an eyebrow in her direction—as if a piece of furniture had suddenly grunted—turning her attentions back to James immediately, letting it be known she resented the interruptions, touching him with every other word she spoke, as if she had to remind him that she was there.

Although she shouldn't have to bother, Zoe had thought acidly. Someone the size of a sofa, covered in an almost transparent négligé, could hardly be overlooked.

The sight of those long, scarlet painted nails scraping up and down the firm, olive-toned flesh of James' tanned arms had made Zoe's stomach lurch and she'd been actually glad when he'd got to his feet, his tone perfectly pleasant as he suggested, 'Time to go, Zoe. Got everything?'

If he'd noticed Stephanie's deliberate rudeness he wasn't showing it, or letting it bother him; it probably amused him to watch his fiancée put her firmly in her place, Zoe had seethed as she stood up immediately, reaching for her handbag and briefcase with one hand, smoothing down her neat plain skirt with the other.

Her mouth became tight when Stephanie, her simpering little-girl voice sounding ridiculous coming from so large a lady, said, 'I don't see why you have to take her. That dumb driver of yours could do it. But if you must, hurry back, my darling. I've got lovely things planned for us.'

Bitch! Zoe thought, but ignored her, turning her attention to James.

'Do let's get moving!' The look she had given him had been withering. 'I hate wasting time.' Which should let them both know what she thought of them and state her refusal to be a downtrodden doormat.

Expecting a lecture on her lack of respect for her betters, Zoe was surprised to find James affability itself, though she was a little suspicious of the maddening smile that hovered around his utterly kissable mouth.

Kissable! What the heck did she imagine she was thinking about? He had never kissed her and was never likely to. Not that she'd want him to, of course, she muttered self-righteously inside her head. And knew she was lying. And despised herself.

Because up until recently she'd always had total control over her sexuality. Indulging in casual sex was a fool's game and falling in love, making a deep commitment to one person, was another. She had first-hand knowledge of how easily it could lead to betrayal and loss. So she'd sublimated all that latent sexual energy into her career, and had been content.

And would be so again, she assured herself, her mouth tightening, her eyes fixed on the scenery as the road led down through the welcome shade of an olive grove.

Despite this man's cold and calculating character, his unspeakable arrogance, his physical presence was capable of jolting all her peacefully sleeping hormones into wild and wanton life. She had to be honest enough to accept that unpalatable fact, but all she had to do was make sure those demeaning desires weren't ungovernable and hang on to the knowledge that, back in London, absorbed by her career and never having to see him, his startling and unwanted effect on her would become a rapidly fading memory.

Give her a couple of weeks and she'd be able to laugh at this. Give her a couple of months and she'd have completely forgotten what it felt like to want to make love to a man so violently that her very bones trembled inside her.

Determinedly, she made herself make the right noises when he pointed out the heights of the Serra do Caldeirao, a harsh, mountainous area supporting twisted cork oaks and the cultivated area, known locally, he informed her lightly, as *barrocal*, where olive, carob and almond trees flourished.

Normally she would have been fascinated, twisting around in her seat to absorb everything—from the rugged, sun-drenched landscape and the herds of goats at pasture in the fields to the occasional squat white farmhouse—but now she could only wish the journey over and done with and hope she was coming across as being politely interested and that he would put her patches of abstraction down to the fact that her mind was on the working day ahead.

She was almost ready to weep with relief when he eventually drew up in the factory car park on the fringe of Loule and actually shuddered when she stepped out of the car into the blazing sunlight. She closed her eyes briefly, hating her reaction to him. It made her feel fatally out of control. It made her feel stupid. She couldn't bear it!

'Are you all right?'

She forced her eyes open. He was standing over her, towering above her, tossing his car keys from one hand to the other. The silvery eyes were dark with concern, shadowed by silky black lashes. Strange how his eyes could look silver at times, reflecting the white light of the sky, and almost black at others, reflecting emotions she couldn't begin to guess at—didn't want to even try. Stranger still that he could project concern, as if he cared about her well-being...

But then he would, wouldn't he? A sick accountant was no good to him.

He pocketed his keys. He moved closer. A gentle hand came down on her shoulder. It burned through the thin cotton of her blouse, branding her skin, and she bit back a whimper, forced a brilliant, empty smile.

'I'm fine. It's the heat. I'll probably be getting used to it by the time I have to go home.' She shrugged his hand away, wondering what he would think if he knew how his touch affected her, if he could hear the way her blood sang in her veins whenever he was near, if he knew how hard it had been to fight against the instinct to turn to him, touch him... Hard, and growing harder...

'Will your manager have arrived yet?' Not too difficult to get the right impersonal words out, but she had no control over her voice; it was disgracefully husky, but he didn't seem to have noticed.

He tipped a dark eyebrow in the direction of the only other car on the parking area, a low-slung, open-topped sports job.

'As you see. Ben has a weakness for fast cars. And women. You've been warned.' He set off towards one of the doors in the functional modern building and Zoe wondered. Fast cars and women in general? Or fast cars and fast women? Had he been joking? With James it was difficult to tell and she wasn't going to ask because, coming on the heels of that 'warning', she had the idea she wouldn't like the answer.

Ben Bishop was waiting for them in a small modern office off the main one. He looked harmless enough, his reasonably attractive features topped by a thatch of mid-brown close-cropped curls. A bit on the burly side and somewhere in his late twenties, she guessed, and his smile was as warm as his handclasp.

Flushing slightly, she disengaged her fingers from the slightly overlong encounter and cursed the way she immediately and instinctively glanced towards James. The action in itself was much too revealing and her annoyance with herself, and with him, intensified as she saw the grim set of his mouth, his brooding eyes.

Ben was saying something about welcoming her on board, offering all the help she needed, but she wasn't listening. James Cade had no right to scowl like that—as if he had caught his manager and his hired accountant doing something not quite nice behind the filing cabinet!

Had he warned her about Ben's personal preferences because he thought she'd be easy game? If so, it must mean that, despite everything, he still suspected her morals and was probably afraid, given the track record he accorded her, that she would spend the whole of her two weeks here indulging in a torrid affair with his manager rather than properly immersing herself in the on-site audit, checking the fixed assets and stock levels like a good little tax specialist.

Her face went red at the very idea. Yet, she reasoned, if that was the way his mind worked, she'd give him something to fret about! It would be entirely his own fault if his concern over her lack of morals—and the resultant lack of good work she'd put in for his company—made it impossible for him to focus all his mind on keeping his intended bride sweet!

Time would show the quality of her work and she would have the last laugh, so she pointedly ignored all the comments he made, only noting that his tone got satisfactorily terser and terser, and pinned the whole of her seemingly fascinated attention on Ben, smiling softly and batting her eyelashes, nothing too obvious, of course, but obvious enough to give the pompous, holier-than-thou James Cade a dose of profound mental indigestion.

And when he finally decided to leave them to it she said, not taking her eyes from Ben, 'Yes, do hurry. You were told to, remember? Stephanie will be getting withdrawal symptoms.'

The moment the words were out of her mouth she knew she had gone too far. A short while ago the very idea of speaking to a superior that way, in front of another employee, would have been unthinkable.

But her troubled relationship with James Cade made her natural circumspection a thing of the past and, even when his icy silence forced her to look at him and she saw the chilling threat of retribution in his eyes, she couldn't be sorry, and tilted her chin defiantly, not even flinching when the office door closed with a reverberating bang behind him.

Putting her heavy briefcase on the vacant desk, she didn't wonder what Ben Bishop thought of the way she'd suddenly changed from a fatuous, lash-batting bimbo to an ultra-efficient, get-on-with-the-job career person. It didn't matter. Nothing mattered now except the need to prove herself ultimately to James, with the added spice of tormenting him a little along the way.

She sighed now, stacking papers together and pushing them into her briefcase. Time to call it a day. Despite the way James had managed to snarl up her thought processes during the day, she'd put some good work in.

And she had enough paperwork to be going on with to keep her in her room until bedtime; the perfect excuse to avoid spending any time at all with the other two. Standing up, she flapped the neckline of her blouse. It was so hot. Even though Amalia, Ben's secretary, had kept her supplied with iced drinks during the day, she still felt as if she'd spent the last eight hours in a Turkish bath.

At some point during the day she'd lost the pins that had loosely secured her hair and now it tumbled heavily around her face, on to her shoulders. She put her hands up to lift the weight off the nape of her neck and Ben walked through the open office doorway.

Leaning against the frame, his mouth rueful, he told her, 'You get acclimatised in time. But it can be heavy if you're not used to it. You'd have done better to arrange your visit in spring or autumn.' His eyes dropped, flowing down her body, and Zoe lowered her hands smartly, letting her soft pale hair tumble around her face. She turned to collect her briefcase just as he asked, 'Someone meeting you?'

'Yes, Vitor's driving me back, apparently.'

'Pity. I could have given you a lift. Any time. Anywhere. You'd only have to name it.'

'What—in that snarly-looking thing parked outside?' Best to treat his offer lightly. She hadn't liked the way he'd looked her over, as if assessing the quality of the goods, deciding whether he was interested or not. But she didn't want to make an enemy of him because she needed his whole-hearted co-operation if her job was to run smoothly.

So when he grinned and shook his head, telling her, 'It doesn't always snarl, believe me. It and I, both, can be as gentle as pussy-cats when we need to be! Tell you what——' he moved further into the room, coming close, and she wasn't going to back off because that wasn't her style '—cancel tomorrow evening's car and we'll ride down to the coast, have dinner, a few drinks. How about it?'

All she did was keep on smiling and offer, 'We'll see——'

Her rider that she thought pressure of work would make her acceptance of his offer extremely unlikely was strangled at birth when James said from the open doorway, 'Running a night shift, Bishop?'

She didn't blame Ben for tensing up before he slowly turned to face his company's chief executive. There wouldn't be many people who would risk tangling with James Cade. That tone had been hard enough to split rocks, and it didn't soften as he added, 'Did you get me that projected output for the first half of next year? I asked for it this morning, remember?'

Had he asked? Zoe couldn't remember. She'd been too busy trying to pretend she was riveted by each and every word that had issued from Ben's lips to recall a single thing about the ongoing conversation. She shuddered. She wouldn't like to be in the manager's shoes if he had forgotten.

Carefully, she avoided James's hard grey stare, gathered her things and excused herself dulcetly.

'I'll leave you to it. Vítor will be waiting. Night, Ben.' And swept serenely by, inwardly quailing because, as ever, all her senses went on red alert whenever James was near, and all those senses were singing out the fact that, for whatever reason, her temporary boss was in a cold rage. And gulped frantically, her throat closing up, her legs going weak, as a black-shirted arm barred her way through the open doorway.

James said with silky menace, 'Vitor isn't here. Wait in the car until I'm ready,' then stepped aside, letting her go and she went, walking as steadily as she could through the deserted main office, along the empty corridors, past the door to the canteen where she and Amalia had chatted together over a light salad lunch and out by the side door into the car park and the heat of the late afternoon sun.

Another encounter with James had not been what she'd planned for what remained of the day. She'd hoped for a tray in her room and a quiet evening with her paperwork. She hadn't wanted to see the engaged couple again. Either of them.

The car was unlocked but she didn't get in, just leant against the gleaming bodywork hoping the heat of the sun would warm the cold spot deep inside her breast. It was the cold fingers of despair that clutched her heart with such an icy grip, she knew it was. The despairing realisation that she had no weapons with which to fight her reaction to James Cade.

She only had to see him to want to touch him and nothing, not the way he had treated her in the past, her knowledge of the type of man he was, her own natural fastidiousness, could help. And the more she saw him, the more her wretched body cried out for him. It was getting worse.

If only he and Stephanie hadn't elected to spend a holiday at the villa, she mourned, uselessly grinding her teeth. Or if only, having done so, James had kept well away from the factory. If he was going to make a habit of calling in she wouldn't know a moment's peace.

Though he probably needed the diversion, she decided cynically. Though he and Stephanie were obviously lovers, planning to marry, he would regard the time he spent with her as a duty, an insurance for the future. He could be no more in love with his chairman's spoiled daughter than she was!

'Get in.'

The clipped command made every one of her muscles go rigid and she knew if she relaxed them for one moment she would start to shake. She gritted her teeth together as he opened the passenger door, held it, impatience on every line of his face deepening to grimness as she shook her head and forced out raggedly, 'I'm going to spend a couple of hours exploring the town. I'll get a cab to bring me back when I'm ready. And don't wait dinner. I'll get something out——' She clamped her teeth together because she was beginning to babble and was rendered speechless, anyway, when he said decisively, 'No. If you want to explore the area you'll do it with Vitor, or with me. Not on your own, and not with Bishop, either. Understand me? Now get in. I've got something to say to you and you're going to listen. And before you start nattering on about off-duty hours, let me remind you of who I am and warn you that you fully deserve to get what's coming.'

Having her defences cut from under her was no joy. She'd been about to remind him she was free to do as she wished out of working hours. And she had a pretty fair idea of what was coming and besides, his long black-clad legs were planted apart, his pelvis thrust aggressively forward—a menacing male stance if ever she saw one, and one that did her rioting hormones no good at all.

Resigning herself, she slid into the passenger seat and waited defeatedly for him to join her. But she wasn't so far gone in loss of self-esteem to allow him to see how easily he'd won the battle. As soon as he'd joined her, before he'd had time to start the engine, she said coolly, 'Perhaps you're right. You know the area better than I do. Let Vitor know he's to meet me after work tomorrow and he can act as bodyguard, as you apparently believe I need one. Now,' she folded her hands demurely in her lap, 'what was it you had to say to me?'

She fully expected a coldly terse lecture on the subject of insubordination, gross in her case, but all she got was a grim expletive, thankfully drowned out by the savage roar of the engine as he accelerated out of the parking area. And he didn't head for São Bras and the uplands but into the centre of Loule, an attractive town of whitewashed houses, sleeping beneath the sun, castle walls enclosing the old heart of the ancient Roman settlement.

James parked the car in a tiny square and sat staring straight ahead, his body completely still except for his fingers which were drumming against the steering-wheel. Zoe risked a glance at his stony profile then lowered her eyes quickly to her hands, watching the way they twisted together in her lap.

The tension in him was enormous, transmitting itself to her, and she had been tense enough to begin with. Being with him always wound her up. But someone had to say something, to open the way and let him get whatever was bugging him off his chest, and then they could talk about it and she would be cool and serene if it killed her, so she managed calmly, 'Why are we here? I thought you were anxious to get back to the villa.'

As if her mention of the villa—and the woman waiting back there?—opened the floodgates, his fingers stopped drumming and he slewed round in his seat, his face all tight lines as he grated, his voice low and savage, 'I hate the effect you have on me. Sometimes it makes me want to shake you to within an inch of your life! Hardly a safe state of mind to be in when driving. So I'll say what has to be said while the brakes are on. I'll buy you a drink. I don't know about you, but I damned well need one.' He was out of the car even as he spoke and she followed automatically, her mind whirling.

His car might be stationary, but he had no brakes on his emotions right now. And if she could get the coldly calculating chief executive of Wright and Grantham to get all steamed up this way—without even really trying—then perhaps—— But no, she refused to entertain the thought. That way could lie madness, self-delusion, self-destruction...

Her heart was fluttering wildly, nearly completely out of control, her legs shaking weakly as she fought back the treacherous hope that he found her as obsessively affecting as she found him, and she was more than thankful to sink down at a table outside a restaurant on the shady side of the square.

She tried not to look at him as he seated himself opposite her because she was afraid her emotional confusion would show in her eyes. But her eyes were drawn instinctively to his, she could no more stop herself looking at him than she could stop breathing, and saw the threat of punishment deep in the silvery depths and felt her soul shake.

Though not with fear. With something she was unable to name. And at long last he spoke, his voice cold with what she could only describe as dislike, which showed up those earlier, crazy hopes for the ultra-ridiculous things they had been.

'As you know, Zoe, I have reservations about you. Strong ones, despite the hard facts I picked up from your family. It would have been better for my peace of mind had I had you taken off our account, as I'd originally intended. But, having no definite proof to back up my reservations, I didn't, and that being so you must agree that you owe it to both of us to extend an equal fairness to me.'

She owed him nothing! But was too busy hating him all over again to tell him as much. There were other ways of getting her own back. And she sat, prim-mouthed, as he beckoned a waiter and gave his order in rapid Portuguese and when he'd finished she enquired, very politely, 'And how do you see me doing that—other than doing the job I'm paid for to the best of my not inconsiderable abilities?'

He wasn't the only person on this earth who could use arrogance as a weapon. She stared at him coldly, saw the way the dappled light created dark slashing shadows beneath his harshly jutting cheekbones, and looked away quickly, catching her breath, catching her hatred for him and holding on to it tightly because it was her only defence against his powerful physical presence and what it did to her.

Reservations. Wished he'd thrown her off his company's accounts. Which meant that, despite all her explanations, his meeting with her family, he still viewed her as a flawed character. Suspect. A loose woman. An idiot could have worked that much out.

The wine came, white and chilled, creating a film of condensation on the outside of the glasses as it was poured and the waiter put a bowl of plump green olives on the table between them.

When he had gone James told her, 'You can watch that razor you call a tongue for a start. Snipe at me as much as you like in private, you know what I think of you, so I dare say you've the right. But you can cut it out when we're around other people. Understand?'

He looked as if he hated her. Quietly and coldly hated her. The earlier anger had gone, leaving only an icy contempt.

Zoe hid a shudder, picked up an olive and nibbled at it. Two could hate. Two could make stipulations. Besides, she'd been in the wrong, had known it as soon as she'd tossed that remark out in front of Ben this morning. She owed him some sort of an apology and she made it stiffly.

'I shouldn't have told you to hurry back to Stephanie, not in front of Ben. That kind of thing won't happen again. Your—relationship—with that woman is nothing to do with me, or anyone else for that matter.' She lifted her glass and sipped from it, the cold liquid sliding down her throat like silk. She didn't look at him to see how he had taken her less than fulsome apology because she hadn't finished yet. 'And while we're talking about Stephanie, perhaps you could ask her to find some manners from somewhere. She looks at me as if I were something unpleasant she's discovered on the bottom of her shoe. I don't like it. OK? And if that's all, perhaps we could go now? I've got a stack of paperwork I want to get stuck into.'

She had, she thought, won the round. Apologised—stiltedly. Stipulated. Ended the interview. She did look at him then, pushing the mass of hair back off her face, preparing to leave, and thought she saw a gleam of amusement, or maybe even admiration, deep in his eyes.

But must have been hopelessly wrong because he came back immediately, cutting her down to size.

'We leave when I'm good and ready, and not before. And no, that's not all.'

She flicked him a look that was supposed to indicate suppressed impatience, hiding, she hoped, her trepidation. So he had another gripe; well, she could handle that. Whatever. What she couldn't handle was his undiluted company. What it did to her. He made her ache for him, even though she hated the sight of him, and that made her despise herself.

Quickly, her eyes fell from his, fell to his glass, unwillingly drawn to the way those strong, lean fingers were idly playing with the stem. Like the rest of him, they seemed mean and moody, capable of handing out pleasure or pain without changing gear...

'I imagined I'd warned you against having anything to do with Bishop, apart from work,' he said drily. 'Yet I walked in and heard you making cosy little assignations. I'm not asking you to stay away from him socially; I'm telling you.'

'Is that a fact?' Anger made her face go tight. Ben had been trying to make a date and she had been trying to let him down lightly. But Cade wouldn't look at it that way. Cade wouldn't listen to a word she said in her own defence. He hadn't in the past and was obviously not about to start now. He was determined to pick holes in her character, so he could go right ahead. See if she cared!

'A firm fact.' He sounded bored now. Looked bored, too, leaning back in his chair, his eyes shuttered. She'd make him see she wasn't some little dimwit, quaking in her shoes at the very thought of displeasing him.

'And what do you intend to do if I don't see it that way?' She, too, could sound bored. 'Throw me off the job? I don't think your excuse that I spent some of my free time in the company of one of your employees would go down too well, do you?' She drained her glass and refilled it recklessly. 'Besides, I don't see what your objections can be. You say he likes women—so do a lot of men—and I'm old enough to look after myself. And he can hardly be a rapist or he'd have been banged behind bars before now.'

She was well in her stride now, the bored image forgotten, and she wasn't letting him get a word in, not that he tried. He was watching her closely, between half closed eyelids, and she snarled, 'Besides, with your perfect ethics, he wouldn't be in your employ if he went around the countryside ravishing women without their consent.' And before he could tell her that he thought that in her case the consent would be a foregone conclusion, she ripped out, 'And talking of ethics—morals, if you like—are you sure your reasons for proposing marriage to your chairman's daughter are beyond reproach?'

She'd done it now, well and truly, and she didn't care. She stared at him with defiant fury and saw his mouth twitch and wanted to smack him but contented herself with an acid, 'I'm sure you'll be perfectly suited.' And he could make what he liked of that. 'Have you decided on the date?' In the mood she was in right now, she'd mark it in her diary and go along and cheer and clap because their marriage would save another male and female from the utter misery of being tied to either one of them.

'The subject has come under discussion.'

Amazingly, he seemed to be laughing at her. She'd expected him to order her out of Portugal on the next available flight. And 'The subject has come under discussion'! Like a board meeting! Where was the romance in that? Nowhere, and she knew it. Oh, how could he be so calculating, so scheming, so devoid of any human emotion? So empty. No hunger, no wanting...

'The thought of my marriage to Steph really gets under your skin, doesn't it?' he remarked idly, that infuriating smile still playing around the corners of his mouth. 'I wonder why.'

She could have told him that the idea of his marrying for career reasons sickened her, painted him black, and she didn't want to see him that way. Told him that the very thought of him sharing physical intimacies with any woman sickened her even more. But as that was quite out of the question she simply shrugged and said dully, trying to dig herself out of the hole she'd opened up with her own stupidity, 'I can't imagine why you should think I care what you do with your life. I think we should get back to the villa, don't you? I don't want any more to drink.'

She'd already had too much, she recognised sourly. James had barely touched the glass he'd given himself. She'd had all the rest. There was barely an inch left in the bottle. She didn't much like herself at the moment and perhaps he picked that up because he spoke softly.

'Don't look so miserable. Nobody's died. Your mouth's too pretty to droop.' He was raking her features with his silvery eyes, lingering on her lips as if committing the soft pink curve to memory and her heartbeats quickened, everything inside her quickened, coming to searing life, her lips parting as if they were readying themselves for his kiss and he leaned across the table, his arms resting on the top, his voice slow and infinitely seductive as he suggested, 'We've both aired our grievances. Why don't we take a little time to begin again, on an easier footing?'

'Why not?' What else could she say? That she didn't want to stay here a moment longer because he was dangerous? Like this he was dangerous. The hard, contemptuous look was gone, something else in its place. Something she couldn't cope with. Something that was entirely in her imagination, surely? He wanted an end to the sniping, that was all. Why put up with aggro if you didn't have to? 'That's if your fiancée won't mind,' she tacked on belatedly, just to remind herself of the type of man he was and to show him that she couldn't so easily be tricked into losing her defensive prickles.

'You can safely leave the management of my love-life to me.' He was smiling widely now, his strong teeth white and perfect, and she went cold inside because 'management' was the name of the game and love didn't come into it and she blinked, not understanding, when he went on to invite softly, 'So tell me about yours.' Then prodded, making her understand, 'Is there anyone special? Permanent?'

'No,' she answered decisively now, shaking her head, making her pale hair fly around her face. 'I'm not into permanent relationships.' Which had been entirely the wrong way to put it, given his opinions of her. Quickly, she tried to retrench. 'Falling in love can have disastrous consequences. I've seen it happen with my own family, not to mention various work colleagues. I would never put myself in the position of depending on someone else for my happiness.'

She gave him a worried look from beneath defensively lowered lashes, but, far from commenting on her cynicism, he surprised her.

'Then we start out from the same basic premise. Falling in love is a game for fools.' Which was as good as telling her what she already knew, that he wasn't in love with Stephanie Wright. And, looking into the gleaming silver of his eyes she felt an unwilling stab of compassion and before she could swallow them, the words were out.

'Did you have a disastrous love-affair?' Then sank back in her seat because she had given him sympathy once before and had had her head bitten off for her pains, but he simply shrugged those wide hard shoulders.

'I made the usual youthful mistake of believing I was in love. I was seventeen and thought I couldn't live without her. I remained in that preposterous state for all of three weeks. I can't remember her name now and can barely recall what she looked like.'

Hardly traumatic enough to account for his distrust of love. Perhaps his parents had never stopped fighting, maybe he'd been brought up in a battlefield. She wasn't going to ask. She'd trodden on that minefield before. But she was intrigued and perhaps he expected further probing because he put the spotlight on her again, his dark head dipped on one side, his eyes almost cruel in their probing intensity.

'There must be men in your life, surely?'

'Why?'

'Now there's a silly question.' His eyes drifted over her suddenly flushed face, her rumpled hair, down to the open neckline of her shirt. His hand lifted slowly and he took the plain white fabric between his finger and thumb. 'When it suits you, you wear this kind of prim disguise. But it doesn't help, does it? It doesn't hide all that sensuality; it reaches out to swamp a man's senses, you can't control it.'

His eyes were holding hers, telling her something she could barely believe. He found her as physically exciting as she found him.

There was no escape route, no way out, not now. Not now when the needs of her body had anaesthetised her brain. And when his fingers slid below the fabric, with slow and deadly enticement, stroking the inner roundness of her breast, her lips parted on a sigh of weak compliance because the sensation filled the world, excluding her former fastidiousness, excluding the other people seated around them, as if nothing existed, nothing mattered but the way his hand felt as it curled around her breast.

And naked desire hazed her eyes, locking them with his, holding them together in this wildness of sensation, and she lifted her hand, placing it over his, as if to keep it there, always, as if she had known what would happen next.

But even that vaguely formulated prescience couldn't prepare her for the shock of seeing his mouth twist with hard self-disgust, the way he withdrew his hand as if her warm flesh burned like the fires of hell. The way he stood up and walked away, his shoulders rigid, leaving her to gather herself together as best she could and follow on legs that felt like water. Carrying a burden of crushing shame, a burden that could well take her the rest of her life to shrug away.

CHAPTER EIGHT

ZOE followed on legs that threatened to give way beneath her, wishing she could disappear in a puff of smoke and never be heard of again.

How could she have allowed James to—touch her so intimately, to—to fondle her? Allowed it to happen in full view of anyone who might be looking—making all the right encouraging noises, too!

Around him she was helpless, and hopeless. He was like a dark and bitter drug, altering her body chemistry, making her do things that were completely out of character, utterly foreign to her normally fastidious nature.

Nervous looks, slanted from deeply humiliated eyes, assured her that, thank heavens, no one was pointing fingers, disgust or amusement on their faces. A few old men engrossed in their newspapers, young couples engrossed in each other, a pair of harassed parents trying to control their high-spirited children. So no, thank the Lord, her shame had not been noticed. It was only apparent to her. And James.

He was already in his car, the engine ticking over, the passenger door open. Waiting for her, obviously. The idea of travelling back to the villa with him repulsed her. Yet what else could she do? She had neither the strength nor the initiative now to argue with him, find a cab to take her back. She just wanted to creep to her room and keep out of his sight for as long as she could.

Breathing deeply, she tried to gain some control over her emotions. The way they were bubbling and boiling about just now made her feel physically ill, and she was still trying when she slid into the car, psyching herself up to a state where she could counter the spate of unpleasant comments on her demonstrably low moral character she just knew were about to come.

But he said nothing. Grim-faced and silent, he drove at a speed that frightened her silly, left her stomach way behind. Taking no risks though, she assured herself, watching the scenery fly by in a blur through wide green eyes. But he wasn't the type to take risks, was he? Like her, he had openly admitted he would never take the risk of falling in love. Unlike her, though, he was prepared to marry and, presumably, father children, for coldly mercenary reasons.

And he hadn't been taking risks when he'd touched her so intimately back there. 'Just testing'. She could almost hear him say it and closed her eyes as a fresh wave of humiliation engulfed her. Putting his misconceived theories to the test, finding out for himself just how easy she was!

Those erotically moving long fingers of his hadn't been drawn on that voyage of discovery because he hadn't been able to help himself, because she excited him physically—as she had for a moment or two deluded herself into nearly believing. Far from it. The almost indecent haste about the way he'd withdrawn, the look of revulsion on his face, left no room for delusions. He would probably rush to the bathroom the moment they reached the villa, scrub his hands in boiling water and carbolic until no trace of the way her warm, eager body had felt was left to linger in the sensory cells of his skin.

It was, she consoled herself miserably, just as well. If his exploratory touch had been for real, if he'd been as physically drawn to her as she was to him, then her treacherous body would have betrayed her into having an affair with him. A madly consuming, passionate affair, the first of her life, and she would never have been the same again, never been her own woman.

She would have been his. Always. Never able to forget. Despite everything—the man she knew he was, the woman she had believed herself to be—she would have been his. And that would have been fatal, unthinkable.

They reached the villa just in time. She was violently sick the moment she hurled herself into the bathroom adjoining her room. But at least it gave her the perfect excuse to skip dinner.

She had no idea where James was, or Stephanie for that matter, but Isabel was sympathetic.

'It's the heat,' she comforted when she brought a jug of iced juice to the room and listened to Zoe's excuses for skipping the evening meal. 'Why don't you take a shower and get comfy on your bed and I'll bring you something light on a tray?'

And she did: iced vegetable soup and fresh fruit, and the information that Vitor would drive her in in the morning, provided she felt up to work, of course, and also the stonily received, 'The *senhor* and his lady have gone out. Such a beautiful dress she wore—very expensive!' Dark eyes rolled expressively. 'But then you know who her father is? They come here together, just sometimes. He is very wealthy!'

Which was precisely why James Cade had decided to marry his large lady, Zoe thought sourly. Money and position meant power, and Cade was greedy for it. He had to be because he certainly wasn't marrying his chairman's daughter for her exquisite looks and wonderful nature!

She had a sudden, sickening mental picture of James touching Stephanie the way he had touched her earlier and groaned distractedly, shaking her head to dispel the image and Isabel asked quickly,

'You are feeling unwell again? Should I call for the doctor?'

'No. I'll be fine,' Zoe countered at once, adding beatedly, 'Thanks. But there's nothing wrong that an early night won't put right.' And there was nothing wrong with her that a doctor could cure. They didn't prescribe pills and potions for shame and deep self-disgust. She was going to have to cure herself, so to begin with she volunteered, 'James said I might explore the area, provided Vitor was with me. What do you think? Would Vitor be free tomorrow evening, after work? Would he mind if he drove me to the coast perhaps? We could eat out; it could be fun.' It could also be the only way to save her from the awful humiliation of spending any time at all with James, knowing that every time he looked at her he would be seeing the look of ecstasy on her face, the look he had conjured with the magic of his hands.

'My brother will be glad to,' Isabel assured her. 'I'll let him know what you suggested, shall I?'

And that was that. If she skipped breakfast—and the way her stomach was feeling right now that would be no hardship—and she kept Vitor out late, or reasonably so, she could well avoid James for a full twenty-four hours. After that, she'd think of something, and if there was any problem with Vitor devoting his time to chauffeuring her around during the coming weekend she'd hire a car.

That settled in her mind, she called forth the sane and
sensible part of herself, the part that James Cade had
pushed into oblivion, and spread the papers she'd
brought home with her out on a convenient table beneath one of the windows and worked until her eyes
would no longer stay open without the benefit of
matchsticks.

Even so, late as it was, she couldn't sleep. She hadn't
heard the others return. Though why that should keep
her ears straining for the sound of his car she couldn't
imagine. He was vile, a scheming, cruel monster, and
she didn't care where he was or what he was doing, or
who he was doing it to. Come to think of it, and viewed
objectively, even Stephanie was far too good for him.

In the event, she didn't have to make wild plots to avoid
the humiliation of having to see James. He was never
around at breakfast-time although Stephanie always was
supplying the information that darling James had risen
early, gone for a walk in the hills. It was his habit, he
found strenuous walking the best way of keeping fit.

And at least the other woman was talking to her now,
not much, but some, and always about James. Darling
James this, darling James that, until Zoe decided she'd
preferred it when Stephanie had totally ignored her.

So James must have had a tactful word in his bride-
to-be's ear, keeping his side of the bargain. And Zoe was
given no opportunity to be less than respectful in front
of other employees because four days had gone by
without him turning up at the factory, checking on her
or whatever.

And Ben Bishop hadn't tried to date her, either,
treating her with careful politeness which was fine as far
as Zoe was concerned except it meant that James must

have used his position of total authority to warn him off. And he certainly hadn't done that because he was afraid his womanising manager might corrupt her sweet, girlish innocence! Oh, no—James was firmly convinced that in this case the boot was firmly on the other foot, that she would lead Ben Bishop astray!

Zoe gnashed her teeth and glared at her reflection. The grey cotton shirtwaister she had chosen to wear this morning successfully repressed all the sensuality she hadn't known she possessed until James had pressed some invisible button and brought it all to wicked life. The staid and sensible garments she had always automatically chosen now seemed like little grey lies, falsifying her true nature, making her yearn to clothe herself in sensuous silks, soft lace and dreamy chiffon, in vibrant jewel-like colours that would emphasise all that was exotic in her.

Yet that couldn't be the truth, either. She tore suddenly troubled green eyes from her reflection and, soft lips compressed, reached for her handbag and briefcase. She wasn't exotic, and sensual was a word that had never entered her head until James had shattered her composure with all that devilish sexual chemistry.

So maybe the truth lay somewhere in between. Maybe she would never go back to being completely cool and sensible—sort of sterile—again and maybe falling in love would bring that hidden sensual side of her nature to blazing, glorious life, making her forget her deep reservations regarding emotional commitment.

But she wasn't falling in love, she howled inside her head. She wasn't! She couldn't. She wouldn't—not with a man like James who was cold and scheming and utterly heartless. And who thought she was a tramp!

She had already decided to skip breakfast. Listening to Stephanie go on and on about James Cade's perfections, which, as far as Zoe was concerned, had to be pure figments of a very strange imagination, was something she could well do without. So she walked quickly through the house, the heels of her sensible shoes making decisive patterns of sound on the cool marble slabs, echoing the no-nonsense mood she was busily imposing on herself, and outside to where Vitor had the car waiting.

It was another beautiful morning, quite perfect, warm and clear and scented with pine and orange blossom and the elusive hint of lavender, the sky lazily blue as it always was until the sun rose high in the heavens and burned it white.

As Vitor came round to hold the door for her, a huge smile flooding his weatherbeaten, attractively ugly features, Zoe grinned right back at him, feeling better by the moment as she fished a notepad out of her bag.

They'd enjoyed a few excursions together, a growing sense of companionship making vocal communication unimportant as he'd ferried her into Loule— accompanying her as she pored over the goods on offer in the many craft workshops, taking her on a tour around the old castle walls which gave her a breathtaking view of the lovely town before guiding her to one of the excellent restaurants where they'd eaten together in easy silence.

And then on another evening he'd driven her up into the mountains and she'd loved every minute of it, and Isabel had packed a picnic supper and, that particular evening, she recalled, James had been waiting when they'd returned. Waiting and watching, not saying word, his dark features brooding, and she'd been thankful to escape to her room because whatever his thoughts had been, they hadn't been pleasant.

Ruthlessly pushing the memory aside, she began to sketch quickly on the notepad, Vitor watching with flattering interest over her shoulder.

No need for the spoken word in any language when she could draw little pictures. When she'd wanted him to take her into the hills a very basic rendering of a car with an arrow coming out of the windscreen pointing towards a mountain range that a child of ten might have been ashamed of producing had been more than sufficient.

Her notepad was filling up with their pictorial communications, some of which had made both of them roar with laughter on more than one occasion, and now, having drawn her ridiculous car heading back to the villa because she intended to work on the ledgers tonight, she was trying to draw 'tomorrow'.

And had got as far as a stylised bed, complete with moon, was busy on two stick people, to be followed by the full circle of the sun and then by something she could only hope would look like a beach and a picnic basket, when the extra sense she'd developed since she'd been around James made her fingers go still and her spine go rigid.

He was approaching along the sweeping drive, his long-legged stride bringing him irrevocably closer, the swing of his wide, strong-boned shoulders intimidating, making her shudder. And, as always, her heart flipped over when she saw him, twisted and tightened in that sudden, fateful and unanswerable moment of deep physical recognition, her flesh helplessly welcoming yet wary, too, and scared.

Yet what woman wouldn't acknowledge his dark attraction? she derided silently. In a black T-shirt and narrow, stone-coloured jeans, his sturdy boots dust-covered, his dark hair damp with perspiration, he looked what he was—a sensational male animal. Yet she could see beneath the strong physical magnetism, she could see the bleakness of his dislike in the cold silver of his eyes, in the bitter and mistrusting slashing line of his mouth.

Heard it in his voice, too, when he demanded, 'Give that to me.'

He took the innocuous notepad from her suddenly shaky fingers, his moodily narrowed eyes on her clumsy drawings, and he probably thought—putting his own twisted interpretation on the moon, the bed and the two people—that she'd been merrily propositioning the still grinning Vitor!

Not 'probably', but definitely, she thought on a wave of near-hysteria as she noted the pinched look of disgust around his finely cut nostrils, and her voice shook with it as she blurted, 'I know what you're thinking. But I'm not asking Vitor to share my bed!'

'Why not?' He thrust the notepad at her. 'You asked me. I recall the occasion vividly.'

The chilling lack of inflexion in his tone made her toes curl in her sensible shoes. She couldn't call him a liar and trying to explain would be a waste of breath, besides being pointless because he was determined to think the worst of her. And she, it seemed, was equally determined to nurture his degrading opinions because, no matter how unwittingly, she always seemed to be doing and saying things that would make those opinions more deeply entrenched!

The battle to make him view her differently was hopelessly one-sided. She kept handing him lethal weapons on a silver plate. Turning away, she got into the car, leaving James and Vitor signing to each other and she could just imagine the information James was conveying, painting her as a wicked little wanton, warning him, destroying the nice casual friendship they'd built.

James Cade was a destroyer, she thought grimly, then reminded herself that she had only another week to get through before she could scurry back to England and begin the process of settling back into her nice, tidy little life and forgetting the destructive physical needs the wretch had woken in her.

And when Vitor joined her she would be able to tell whether or not he gave any credence to what James had been telling him. Although there was no way they could communicate in any language whatsoever she would be able to tell from his body language, by the way he looked at her. Or didn't look at her.

But Vitor didn't join her. James did. Sliding behind the wheel and slamming the door shut, every line of his body tense before he visibly gathered himself, made himself relax and started the engine.

'There are things I have to catch up on at the factory,' he told her brusquely. 'You won't be needing Vitor's services at all today. And from what he conveyed, you were intending to get stuck into some paperwork back at the villa this evening.'

'Suits me.' She shrugged slim shoulders, the gesture eloquently uninterested, she hoped. She did mind James driving her. His presence was torment. But he wasn't going to know that. Besides, 'I hope he also conveyed that I wasn't trying to drag him into my bed.' No sign of uninterest in her tone now. It was hot and rough and

probably betrayed her hurt, because he gave her a shor
sideways glance before swinging the big car out on t
the road, his dark brows slightly bunched, as if her re
sponse had puzzled him.

But he didn't comment. He probably thought makin;
an answer would be beneath his dignity. And he wasn'
dressed for the office, he had obviously been returnin;
from one of those long, strenuous walks Stephanie ha
told her about. He was going to a lot of trouble to kee;
Vitor out of her clutches, she thought with hollov
cynicism. And what about his fiancée? Stephanie woul
be waiting for him to join her for the usual poolsid
breakfast. She'd be wondering where he'd got t(
worrying...

'Won't Stephanie wonder what's happened to you'
she asked tartly, reminding him of his lack of consider
ation, and he shot her down in flames, taking even th
small comfort of putting him in the wrong for once awa
from her.

'Vitor will convey my plans to Isabel, who will, i
turn, verbalise them for Steph. And I'm sure she'll t
able to occupy herself quite happily while I'm away. She
a big girl now.'

In more ways than one! Zoe wriggled tetchily in h«
seat. He was so all-fired arrogant, had an answer f(
everything, and she wondered whether to tell him th.
he needn't have gone to all this trouble to save Vit(
from her promiscuous, predatory clutches then thoug]
better of it. Why waste her breath? She stared straig]
ahead and sighed, and felt, rather than saw, the way I
turned and looked at her before concentrating on t]
road again, and wondered if she was imagining thin;
when he said quietly,

'Why don't we try for a truce?'

Her immediate reaction was one of gut-wrenching relief but she stiffened up her mental processes rapidly; she wasn't going to fall at his feet, squirming with gratitude. So she said stiffly, 'Fine. But might I remind you that I wasn't the one to start all the aggro?' And wondered if she'd been too snippy when he drew the car to the side of the dusty road and cut the engine.

Veiling the niggle of apprehension with the sweep of long lashes, she gave him a questioning look. Another cutting lecture on the inadvisability of answering back, on her failure to show proper gratitude and respect?

She was perfectly capable of ramming the words back down his throat, metaphorically speaking, but was suddenly tired of fighting him.

Looking at him, at the harsh features that were somehow softened, probably by the shade of the twisted branches of the shade-giving cork oak at the side of the road, she felt the sting of tears behind her eyes.

Not only was she weary of fighting him, she recognised, but she wanted the peace of his friendship and approval, too. And even more than that, she wanted the magical wildfire of his love...

She turned her head quickly, unwilling to let him see the betraying shimmer of tears, the soft trembling of her mouth and he turned sideways in his seat, extended a hand to touch her then almost instantly withdrew it as having second thoughts. But his voice coiled softly round her, touched with self-mockery and, perhaps, something much deeper, something she couldn't name, could only sense as tiny shivers tumbled all the way down her spine.

'Point taken. There's a chemistry somewhere that makes us want to smack each other—hardly sensible and definitely not adult. I suggest we try to ignore it. For

my part I think it's because I'm up against the enigma
of your personality—seduction and sensual invitation
on the one hand, a prickly bundle of prunes and prisms
on the other.' The hard mouth curved in a mocking smile.
'I don't like things I can't understand. I hate feeling at
a disadvantage. You'll accept my apology?'

And what could she say to that? She could only agree,
especially when there was not even the tiniest hint of the
feral about his normally tigerish smile. Just warmth and
a glorious openness, and she nodded, too choked to
speak, and he held her eyes with the glittering silver pen
etration of his, his gaze intensifying, enthralling her
telling her something that made her poor heart turn
somersaults, made her breath come quickly, choking her

Her soft lips parted in utter self-betrayal, the way he
body swayed helplessly towards his a tacit admission of
her awareness of his overwhelming, powerful physica
attraction, and she saw something flare in the depths of
his eyes, just fractionally, before his mouth tightened
and his head turned away.

'And that's another thing,' he said coolly as he
straightened and refired the engine, pulling out on to the
empty road. 'That chemistry—whatever—might make
us want to smack each other, but it also makes us want
to leap into bed. Strange?' He gave her a momentar
glance, one black brow querying upwards as if inviting
her opinion, her agreement that it couldn't have been
stranger, then said levelly, as if the matter were of no
great importance, 'Speaking for myself, it's the last thing
I need. And I'll give you the benefit of the doubt and
believe you don't want it, either. So we ignore it and
will go away. And in the meantime we behave politely
like the well-balanced adults we are, for what remain
of your time here. OK?'

Zoe didn't even bother to nod her agreement, but stared unseeingly ahead for the rest of the drive into town. He had admitted the relentless physical attraction between them and he might try to ignore it, as she had done. But it wouldn't go away, as she knew to her cost. And it might be the last thing either of them wanted or needed but it was there, full-blooded, vibrant, insistent, and, for her part, showing scant respect for sanity or common sense.

How long could either of them deny it?

How long would either of them want to deny it?

CHAPTER NINE

'A SHOWER'S called for, don't you think? Followed by something long and cold and thirst-quenching,' James suggested, his eyes on the rear of the heavily laden donkey cart ahead as the big car inched slowly along the narrow, tortuous road to the villa.

'That sounds lovely,' Zoe agreed smoothly, envying his lack of tension. She'd expected him to be muttering under his breath at the hold-up, drumming his fingers impatiently against the wheel. But ever since that revealing talk on the way into work this morning he had been perfectly relaxed, working closely with her in quiet harmony, even seeming to take genuine pleasure in her efficiency, as if the lists of figures she produced had a special language of their own, allowing them to discover an avenue of real communication. It was as if, having got everything out into the open, admitting that he lusted after her, the problem no longer existed.

It hadn't worked that way for her. Trying to act as if the chemistry between them was an irritant she was able to ignore as successfully as he did had left her feeling like a lettuce that was several weeks past its sell-by date. How could she ignore it when it haunted her, filling her thoughts, controlling her dreams, making her body ache to be possessed by his? The strength of her feelings terrified her.

'Followed by a cold finger-supper by the pool.' James spoke softly into the slow silence and Zoe clutched at her lifeline, the bulging briefcase on her lap, and declined thinly.

'I'll pass on that. I'll have a tray in my room and get on with some work.' Being near him was becoming more of a torment with every day that passed. He might enjoy displaying the strength of character that enabled him to ignore the wild fever of wanting, but she didn't have that kind of control.

'No more work until Monday, and that's an order.' The edge in his voice betrayed the fact that he wasn't as relaxed as she had believed, and she twisted her lower lip between her teeth as he added coldly, 'The way you spend all your free time out of the villa, or shut up in your room on the pretext of work, the way you leave a room if I enter it, hasn't gone unremarked.'

The road was a little wider now, the cart edging off towards one side, and in a moment or two he would be able to pass and they'd be back at the villa in no time at all and there were things that had to be said. Stephanie must have commented on the way she had carefully avoided him, but she hadn't been the only one playing that game.

'You haven't come looking for my company, either,' she reminded as he accelerated past the cart and casually saluted the old man who was walking at the donkey's head.

'Exactly. And we both know why,' he countered levelly. 'And so will anyone else with the ability to put two and two together, especially if we can't act naturally over the weekend.' The car was progressing at a speed that sent up a cloud of dust and she was trying to find a counter-argument that would hold water, and couldn't, when he remarked lightly, 'Did I tell you Taylor phoned to say he's coming to check work in progress? His flight got in at midday and he was hiring a car in Faro, so he'll be well and truly settled in by now.'

The subject was closed, so he was changing it. And no, he hadn't told her Luke was coming, and he knew damn well he hadn't. He was letting her know that he expected her to behave as if there were no dark, swirling undercurrents between them because, apparently, Stephanie had already made a comment or two and Luke Taylor was astute enough to put two and two together and come up with precisely the right answer.

For a moment or two Zoe stayed where she was as James parked the car in front of the villa and got out, contemplating the coming weekend with dismay. How could she pretend everything was hunky-dory, as bland as apple pie, when her emotions were in such chaos? How could she, when the potent force of his presence sparked off this unprecedented need, the disintegration of all her moral fibre?

'Zoe?'

He was holding the door open, dark brows bunched, the shaft of concern in his brooding eyes not for her as a human being battered by a devastating whirlwind of the senses, but for the way she would handle herself over the next couple of days. And that view was reinforced when she answered, 'Fine,' slapped an insincere social smile on her face and got nimbly out of the car, quite determined now to show she could be as two-faced as he, hiding her feelings beneath a smooth façade as if they were something to be ashamed of.

Which, of course, they were.

And she recognised his feather-smoothing tactics as he paced by her side as she sailed, as if blithely, towards the villa, asking her, 'Have you been in touch with your family since you got here? I only met them once but even I can recognise closeness when I see it.'

Which was another way of warning her off, telling her that being close in any meaningful way with anyone wasn't how he'd been programmed. Which was a waste of effort because she already knew that. Marrying his chairman's ghastly daughter because it would be a good career move, put even more power in his hands, was as close as he would ever get to anyone.

'Not yet.' She answered his question lightly, pushing away the pointless need to know what had made him the way he was because knowing wouldn't make any difference, would it?

'Phone home whenever you feel like a chat. Let me know how your father's getting along with his baby-sitting companion. Devotion's a rare commodity, but it's past time he understood that having a good relationship with someone else wouldn't degrade what he once had with your mother.'

Which was precisely what she and Petra believed, but what would he know about devotion, or good relationships for that matter? And it was impossible to tell whether his smile was sincere or not because, as they came out of the bright sunlight into the shadows of the coolly paved hall, nothing seemed clear. But he sounded sincere as he added, 'I liked your father. He reminded me of mine. He wanted to teach—he had an enormous empathy with children. But he met my mother and I was on the way before he could take his place at university. He had no family left to speak of, certainly no parents with money to stake him, so he took a job stacking supermarket shelves, married her and gradually worked his way up to manager of the local branch. Like your father, he knew all about devotion to duty.'

His voice had been low, the words spilling out. And now he was silent; no sound at all but the rapid pattering of her heartbeats and the chattering of the cicadas in the grounds outside. Accustomed to the interior dimness now, she could see the return of tension to his driven features, the impatience—not with her this time but with himself. He probably couldn't understand why he had told her anything at all about himself.

He had once harshly warned her off asking any questions about his family background, so did that brief glimpse into his past mean he was beginning to trust her a little?

Her throat went dry just thinking that way. She mustn't give herself any kind of hope at all. It was too dangerous. She'd allowed herself to become besotted enough on the starvation diet of no hope at all.

'I'll take that now.' Her voice was strained with the effort of sounding controlled as she held out her hand for the briefcase he'd carried in from the car. But he shook his head, his frown easing away, demonstrating his cool insistence on the way things were to be.

'I'll put it in a safe place until Monday morning. No work this weekend—we spend it relaxing, remember?'

And how the heck was she supposed to relax? she muttered to herself as she went straight to her room without another word and stripped off her wrinkled shirtwaister.

When she'd imagined the way she felt about James had been her own secret it had been bad enough, forcing her to avoid his company like the plague. So how could she spend the whole weekend with the engaged couple, watching Stephanie fawn over him, cling to him so possessively even as she remembered the way he'd told her he wanted to bed her, telling her he knew she wanted it too. And she hadn't denied it.

Hot tears stung her eyes and spilled over and she wiped them away with the back of her hand, an angry gesture that strengthened her resolve. She marched into the bathroom and turned on the shower and stood under the welcome spray until she'd forced some sense back into her head.

Although James had admitted the attraction, he had told her quite explicitly that he didn't need it. It was an irritant and best ignored. Which he had patently proved he could do.

Well, so would she!

Ignoring the uncomfortable inner voice which reminded her that she had monumentally failed in that respect on all her earlier attempts, she selected a cool gauzy white cotton skirt, topped it with a sleeveless black button-through blouse and rough-dried her hair, leaving it to fall in a cloudy drift of pale blonde silk around her shoulders.

She resisted the temptation to slap on the disguise of make-up—it was far too hot—and consoled herself with the knowledge that Luke would be around. She would stick to him like glue, catch up with all that was going on back at the office. And there would be plenty to tell him about the work in progress here. It would all help to take her mind off James.

Luke's visit couldn't have come at a better time, she told herself as she left her room. He never checked up on her work, leaving her to get on with it, content with picking up the major part of the kudos when it was completed. But the Wright and Grantham account was a new one, and very prestigious, so maybe the need to make sure she wasn't running into problems had been a small part of his decision to pay a brief visit.

But the major reason would have been a few days in the sun, tax-deductible expenses defrayed by Halraike Hopkins, free from the family encumbrances that might cramp his style!

The way she could read Luke like a book brought a smile to her lips and it was still there when she walked into the main salon and found him—white shorts and shirt and a large gin and tonic—lounging on an over-stuffed sofa just inside the open french windows.

'Zoe, my sweet!' He grinned, raising his glass to her. 'How the lack of severity suits you—I always knew you'd be a stunner if you could ever prise yourself out of those battle-dresses you button yourself up in. Come and join me—unless you'd prefer to go fry around the pool. Steph's out there, watching James swim. I can smell the boiling lard from here.'

'Don't be vile!' She made pouring herself a long cool drink the excuse for turning her back on him, hiding her twitching mouth, but Luke, obviously in holiday mood, was not to be chastened.

'Simply stating the obvious. The woman's gross. Nasty-natured with it. I told you she was a bitch, re-member? Can't imagine how Cade can bring himself to——'

'I don't think that's any of our business, do you?' Zoe interrupted hastily. She couldn't bear to think of James touching his fiancée—or any other woman, come to that. It hurt too much.

She turned, smiling fixedly to hide the pain, clutching her glass of chilled orange juice tightly because her hands were suddenly shaking.

Luke moved his feet from the end of the sofa and invited, 'Sit down and tell me how the job's going, then. Needless to say, I have every confidence in you. You wouldn't be in the position you are if I didn't. But it was my excuse for grabbing a few days of luxury.'

'You think I haven't already guessed that?' Zoe sat, grinning at him, more than happy to talk about her work because it would take her mind off James and the shattering effect he had on her, and bit her lip savagely when his voice came from right behind her.

'That's what I like to see. People getting together and enjoying themselves.' His voice was harsh, belying his words. He sounded as if finding the two of them together, sitting close, laughing, disgusted him.

Did he still believe she was a promiscuous trollop? He'd once asked if Luke knew about the supposedly double life she led and had accused her of sleeping with her boss to keep him quiet!

The sheer horror of the supposition brought her head round, troubled green eyes locking with the silver ice of his. The look of furious distaste was confirmation enough and she closed her eyes because she couldn't bear it, and the wretch was naked apart from minuscule black bathing briefs, his superb, hair-roughened, rangy body glittering with droplets of water, the white towel he had slung around his neck contrasting sharply with the olive tones of his skin.

He was as sinfully tempting as the devil himself; he filled her with unbearable longing and, before she knew what was happening, she felt hard, cool fingers beneath her chin, heard the husky concern in his voice as he said, 'What the hell have you done to yourself!'

Her eyes winged open, shocked by the force of what his slightest touch could do to her and met the darkening concern of his, glittering through those thick black lashes. He was hunkered down in front of her, his face mere inches from her own, and her lips parted on an involuntary moan and she tasted the salt of her own blood and realised she hadn't known how sharp her teeth were.

Realised, too, as he gently dabbed at her torn lower lip with the edge of his towel, that she loved this man. For better, for worse, for always. No matter what.

All the safety measures, the barriers she had erected against ever making an emotional commitment, had fallen away like the rags of defeat, blown to tatters by the storm force of finding the one man she would follow, barefooted if need be, to the very ends of the earth—to heaven or hell, it made little difference.

Great green eyes glittered with the hot sting of tears and James murmured with curling amusement, 'Don't cry, baby! You'll live.'

She shook her head in instinctive denial and the tears spilled and he stroked them away with the ball of his thumb, his fingers curved around the fragile bone of her jaw. And she couldn't tell him she wasn't a child, crying because her mouth was sore, that she wept because the wrong man had claimed her love, a man who had cynically admitted that falling in love was a game for fools, who had dispassionately admitted that he lusted after her body but could ignore it because it was a nuisance, like an itch.

And she was almost glad when Stephanie's complaining voice broke the long, timeless moment of sharply sweet intimacy, twisting her head away from James' hands to meet the sharp suspicion in his fiancée's heavily made-up pale blue eyes.

'I thought you were fetching me a drink. What's going on?'

'Let me.' Luke was on his feet, making another break in the gossamer fabric of the moment Zoe had shared with the shatteringly new knowledge of her love for James, with his unprecedented gentleness. She had forgotten he was in the room. For that small fragment of time James had been the only other person in the whole wide world.

And bleak despair muscled in, finally destroying the remnants of that moment as James rose to his full, intimidating height, his face hard and shuttered, and Stephanie, tearing her eyes from Zoe's ashen face, spoke sharply.

'No. Not that!' And she waded over the room to snatch the jug of orange juice from Luke's hand. 'Mix me a dry martini—very dry.'

'Shaken, not stirred?' Luke asked, his face very bland, and earned himself a withering look and an impatient,

'James knows how I like it.' Her head twisted round. 'Where's he got to?' Small pale eyes glared at Zoe, as if accusing her of spiriting him away.

She shook her head wearily. 'To get dressed, presumably.' And held the cold exterior of her glass against her swollen lower lip and wished with all her aching heart that she were safely back in England, looking for that place of her own, enjoying her work, her friendship with her colleagues. Wishing she'd never set eyes on James, wishing she weren't embroiled in this wild emotional upheaval.

'Nobody bothers to dress in this heat. We are very private, after all.' She accepted the glass Luke offered her, not bothering to give him a thank-you, the derision in her eyes saying plainly what she thought of Zoe's modest skirt and blouse. 'And there's no point skulking around indoors. Come outside, I want to work on my tan.'

Zoe wearily complied with the royal command, but Luke muttered some excuse and took himself and his generously freshened drink off somewhere. And, following, Zoe wondered whether someone should tell her that, being so billowy, she shouldn't wear such a disgracefully small bikini. Glittery gold lamé, too, clashing horribly with all those acres of bright red skin.

But she decided her advice wouldn't be welcome, let alone heeded. Why should Stephanie care? She didn't need to look good, or cultivate a pleasant personality, to hook a husband as gorgeous as James Cade, not when she had Daddy's powerful position as bait.

That particular thought did nothing at all to cheer Zoe up and she sank down on a poolside lounger, in the shade of a palm umbrella, and averted her eyes from the unlovely sight of Stephanie rubbing sunscreen over her scorched flesh.

The surface of the pool was blue and limpid and if things had been different she would have enjoyed a lazy swim. As it was, she felt too weary, too drained by her emotions to make the effort, and couldn't even raise an objection, find an excuse, when Stephanie, finished with her sunscreen, sprawled out opposite her and imparted,

'We're all going to the coast tomorrow. It's a long-standing invitation from Claudia Oliveira. When she heard you and your colleague were here—James's doing, not mine,' she disclaimed airily, 'she insisted on your inclusion. Senhora Oliveira is a special friend of Daddy's. When her husband died three years ago she was left a wealthy woman. So I don't have to worry about her being on the make, do I?' She finished her drink in one long swallow and put the empty glass down on the tiled pool surround. 'I've been everything to Daddy since Mummy died. He won't feel so lonely when I marry James if he and Claudia get together.'

'No, I suppose not,' Zoe said, trying to take an interest, trying to suppress the wicked renewal of pain at the thought of the forthcoming marriage. But she had no real interest in the conversation and didn't know why it was taking place, unless Stephanie was trying to be friendly.

She had to force herself to ask, 'When are you and James getting married?'

'Oh, some time next spring,' the other woman said airily. 'The poor boy's very eager, he'd like it to be sooner. But you know how it is—so much to plan. I haven't yet decided who to go to for my dress and my trousseau—and I won't ask your advice,' she trilled; 'I don't want to hear a chain store! Besides, I want to see Daddy settled, preferably with Claudia. Did I tell you he's coming to join me and James? He would have been here this week, but I knew you'd be coming so I put him off. I want him to be able to really relax. He works so hard, poor love.'

Making it sound as if she, Zoe, was a loud-mouthed irritant, getting in everyone's hair, disrupting the peace when she'd done everything possible up until now to keep out of the way. And this socialising weekend hadn't been her idea. Far from it!

Isabel and Vitor were setting dishes of cold food on the terrace table and Zoe wondered if she could make her escape and offer to help them, but Stephanie obviously wanted to continue their unedifying chat.

'Apparently your father's on his own, too.'

An innocuous remark. It might even be construed as sympathetic, so why, then, did those pale eyes gleam with malice? Zoe wondered, correcting her softly.

'Not really. My sister lives with him.'

'So James said. Fascinating. Now how did he get to meet your father, I wonder? He was a schoolteacher, I hear, but James couldn't have met him through school— I don't suppose your father taught at Ludgrove or Winchester or Oxford!' Again the trill of unamused laughter and Zoe got to her feet, controlling her temper.

'Why don't you ask him? If he wants you to know where he met my family, I'm sure he'll tell you.'

James was emerging from the villa, clad now in dark jeans, a loose white shirt tucked into the narrow, belted waistband, closely followed by Luke. Zoe escaped to help Isabel and got through the rest of the evening, somehow, and went to bed still thinking.

Her initial annoyance at the way James had obviously discussed her background with Stephanie—no doubt because she had been probing—had been tempered by the knowledge that he had given very little away; he certainly hadn't relayed the fraught circumstances that had led to his meeting her family.

But Stephanie's remarks about her father's relatively humble position in the education world puzzled her. Boys didn't attend Ludgrove and Winchester unless they were future high-flyers with great wealth behind them. And on James's own admission his parents must have been desperately hard-up when they'd married so young because he was on the way. So where had the money come from to pay for such an expensive education?

She punched her pillow and tried to sleep. What did it matter how he got his education? His father might have played the stock market and made a fortune, for all she knew, and she was perfectly well aware that James Cade's background was of the supremely elevated variety, her own very humble by comparison—she didn't need Stephanie to point it out...

She woke feeling distinctly edgy and got out of bed and began pacing the luxurious room, her arms hugging her body. A whole day in the company of James and his lady was a terrible prospect.

When she'd believed the attraction had been merely physical, and very one-sided, spending any time with him had been difficult enough. But now she had to face the knowledge that she had done what she had always vowed she would never do—fallen deeply and hopelessly in love. And not sensibly, either, but with a man who, although he had admitted to the sexual chemistry, was controlled enough to ignore it because he was determined, above all else, to marry his chairman's daughter!

How crazy could a girl get?

Suddenly her mind was made up. Hurriedly she dressed in jade-green shorts and a matching halter top, twisted her hair up on top of her head and marched out of her room.

She found the others around the breakfast table and announced firmly, addressing Luke, not even sparing James a glance, 'I've decided to get on with some work today. If I put in a few extra hours I could get finished up here ahead of schedule and get back to London. There's plenty of work waiting back at the office.'

She refused to react when she felt the power of James's icy eyes, so sure Luke would agree and back her up. He

had often accused her of being a workaholic but knew
he applauded her dedication to her job.

Even when James said coolly, 'Claudia is expecting
both of you. Surely you wouldn't be so ill-mannered as
to insist you and Luke stay behind to pore over a bunch
of figures?' she still expected Luke to give her the go-
ahead and ground her teeth together in frustration as
Luke agreed,

'Work can wait until Monday. I, for one, am looking
forward to the outing and it's time you learned how to
relax and have fun.'

'Let her stay here if she wants to. I can't see that it
matters. Claudia won't turn a hair if she doesn't turn
up—she doesn't know her from Adam and only in-
cluded her out of politeness.' Stephanie was the only
person backing her up and James got to his feet, his
look unreadable as he answered his fiancée.

'It matters.' And strode away, arrogance in every line
of his tall, rangy body.

Zoe choked down a vulgar expletive, muttered,
'Excuse me,' and stamped after him.

She caught up with him in the main hallway, her green
eyes stormy, her slender body quivering with pent-up
emotions, feeling marginally better as she allowed some
of them to spill out.

'Why are you being so pig-headed about this?' she
demanded hotly. 'Stephanie's got a valid point. Senhora
Oliveira wouldn't be upset if a couple of strangers didn't
turn up at her home today. She would probably be
relieved!'

'Really?' He thrust his hands into the pockets of his
jeans, his brows slightly raised, cool and aloof, and the

frustration, the pain, of loving this impossible man spilled over as she spat,

'You like to see lesser mortals dancing to your tune, don't you? You can't possibly actually want to have me and Luke under your feet all day!'

'I don't "want" Taylor anywhere.' A gleam of unholy amusement glittered in the burnished silver of his eyes. 'And you know where I want you—and it isn't under my feet.'

That reminder, the intensity of the forbidden feelings that surged between them, left her feeling raw and vulnerable and bewildered.

He could actually make a joke of this, treating the way he wanted her with contempt. The sexual chemistry wasn't wanted, as far as she was concerned. Its unwelcome advent must have infuriated him and now he was intent on demonstrating just how easily he could deal with it.

Zoe dragged in a ragged breath. If he could show contempt, then so could she. Praying for a tone of bored sophistication, she tried to match his dismissive attitude.

'You want me in your bed but you're too high-principled to put me there. It might upset your chairman's daughter if she found out, and spoil your plans. Well, I can understand that. But an itch is still an itch, isn't it? And I would have thought you would have preferred the cause of it out of sight and out of mind.'

She was trembling inside at the pain of loving him but her pale, pointed face might have been carved from stone as she watched his features harden, his jaw tighten, an expression of deep self-disgust darken his eyes.

He growled, 'If you and Taylor were here alone you might be out of sight, but you wouldn't be out of mind.

I want you where I can keep an eye on you both.'
He swung on his heels, his wide shoulders rigid. 'The
subject is no longer up for discussion. We leave in
twenty minutes.'

CHAPTER TEN

IT WAS hotter than ever, a heavy, sultry heat that sapped all her energy. More than ever, Zoe wished James hadn't insisted on this.

Claudia Oliveira couldn't have been more welcoming. She was a cheerful, uncomplicated lady who liked everyone to be happy.

'I always had a big party on my birthday,' she explained for Zoe's and Luke's benefit shortly after they'd been introduced. 'Then after my husband died I decided I had nothing to celebrate, but these two insisted on keeping up the tradition, and they were right. Life does go on, isn't that so, my children?'

'And you're the living proof!' Pilar grinned. She was a youthful, slimmer version of her handsome, dark-haired mother; probably a couple of years younger than her brother, Paolo, who was wickedly attractive and well aware of it.

Claudia returned her daughter's smile affectionately. 'That may be so, but with each year I notice that the number of your contemporaries increases while mine diminishes! So take our English guests, find them a drink, and mingle.' She turned to Stephanie. 'I was sad Patrick couldn't make it this year. But your father's a busy man, I know that. He phoned a day or so ago to wish me a happy day and we've made a definite date for next week. For dinner. I will make my special lobster dish, I know how much he enjoys it . . .'

'Come——' Paolo's deep, husky voice cut softly across his mother's conversation as his hand slid beneath Zoe's elbow. 'We will do as ordered and mingle, or perhaps——' black eyes danced '—at the ripe old age of twenty-six I can do as I choose and keep you to myself.'

'Oh, but I——' Zoe was being gently but firmly led over the expanse of browning grass, away from the huge, kidney-shaped pool where most of the guests were. She looked quickly around for Luke but he was deep in conversation with Pilar and a voluptuous redhead in a long flame-red shirt and a tiny black bikini top. No help could be expected from that quarter!

And Paolo was saying persuasively, his hand around her waist now, 'We could play truant. Go down to the village, perhaps. It is lovely and still unspoiled—you must have driven through it on your way up here. Or I could show you around the property. The grounds are extensive—and private—and there's a track over the headland to a tiny cove. No one ever goes there.'

'We have already spent some time in the village,' James cut in suddenly, drily, from just behind them. 'Zoe has been a dutiful tourist and watched the fishermen unloading their catches and had coffee outside a typical bar in a quaint little square. I'm sure that's the type of thing you had in mind, Paolo?' He planted himself in front of them, his stony features quelling, not even pretending to smile as his eyes clashed briefly with hers before turning their freezing intensity back to Paolo. 'As Claudia said, you need to look after your guests. If Zoe wishes to explore the grounds, I can guide her. I've been here before.' Silver eyes mocked the younger man's discomfiture. 'I know my way around.'

'I'm sure you do,' Paolo snapped, his hackles rising, his hand tightening more possessively around Zoe's waist. And he wasn't referring to the extensive grounds that surrounded his family's converted farmhouse. She felt like a bone being tugged between two hungry dogs and she was hating every minute of it.

Incorrigibly flirtatious males such as Paolo she could deal with. What she couldn't cope with was James's dog-in-the-manger attitude. He lusted after her, but that didn't fit into his plans; he wouldn't allow himself to have a brief affair with her—not that she would let that happen, of course—because it might get messy and ruin all his scheming calculations, but he was determined no other man would get the opportunity!

How little he knew her, she thought on a wave of sadness. He still, in his heart of hearts, believed she was a trollop; he had proved that to himself when she had allowed him to touch her, just once, so intimately.

He would never know how he alone had woken all her sleeping sensuality, or that she loved him as she had never believed herself capable of loving. One thing was sure: she would never tell him; her self-respect wouldn't let her. If she were insane enough to blurt out the truth he would never believe her. And even if he did, he would toss her adoration back in her face because he didn't want her. Or only in his bed for the short time it would take to slake his lust.

She made a restless attempt to extricate herself from Paolo's increasingly possessive grasp and almost choked with relief when Stephanie panted up, her face red and shiny, her heavy make-up melting in the heat.

'You might have waited for me,' she grumbled, slipping her arm through James's and giving it a shake. 'I'm dying of thirst. Paolo, go and fetch me a drink while James and I find somewhere shady to sit.'

'Of course.' The handsome Portuguese dipped his head ironically and Zoe thought fleetingly that if his mother married her father Stephanie might find herself being well and truly slapped down for once. The Portuguese male didn't take kindly to being ordered around by his womenfolk and, unlike James, he didn't have to pander at her every whim for what he could get out of her and her father.

Not that she had ever actually seen him pandering to his fiancée, she realised, and he certainly wasn't letting her have all her own way now because when she began to tug him in the direction of a rose-swathed arbour he prised her fingers off his arm and told her, 'Stay here with Zoe. I'll help Paolo with the drinks.' And he walked away, his tall lean body achingly sexy in slim black trousers topped by a white T-shirt which clung like a second skin to the subtly muscled beauty of his upper body.

Zoe's breath caught in her throat. He was so graceful, his movements so fluid. On the surface he was everything a man should be, underneath, though, he was something else entirely. Cruel, cold, calculating. He had a hunk of hewn granite where other people kept their hearts.

An ache of despair tightened her throat. If she had to go against all those former common-sense patterns she'd created for the way she wanted to run her life, and fall in love, why did it have to be with a man like James Cade?

Love was the most uncomfortable, bewildering emotion she'd ever experienced in her life.

'Oh, do come on!' Stephanie said pettishly. 'I'm frying in this sun.'

But it wasn't the sun, Zoe thought, walking listlessly over to the arbour. It was simply the heat, heavy and draining, the sky opaque, a dull grey streaked here and there with ominous splashes of angry crimson. There wasn't a breath of wind.

'I think we're in for a storm,' she remarked, following the other girl to one of the slatted wooden benches. 'We ought to go nearer the house where there's more shelter.'

From here the old farmhouse looked very attractive: cascades of scarlet bougainvillaea covered the sturdy whitewashed walls and beyond the swimming-pool area a brightly striped awning had been erected over one of the long terraces where the buffet tables were laid out. A few people were clustered round the sizzling barbecues but most were cooling themselves off in the pool or lazing around it, and Zoe would rather take shelter up there than be stuck down here with James's fiancée.

'It won't break yet,' Stephanie dismissed, removing her elaborate straw hat and flapping it in front of her face. 'I can't move another inch until I've had that drink.' She pointed to the steps cut into the sides of the terraces. James and Paolo were on their way back. 'And while we're handing out advice, why don't you stop making such a fool of yourself over James? He thought it was faintly amusing to begin with but now it annoys and embarrasses him. If you're not careful you might find yourself taken off the job.'

For a moment Zoe stopped breathing. The implication of what the other woman had said was like a hard blow to the solar plexus. Everything inside her closed up protectively. She felt cold inside, and nauseous. But that was better than being riven by pain. She had been so careful to hide her growing feelings for James, absenting herself as much as humanly possible, keeping out of his way, giving her spiralling desire for him nothing to feed on.

So James must have mentioned the hot, volcanic attraction. Bragging? Letting his fiancée know what a lucky lady she was to have snared him when he only had to look at a woman to have her go weak at the knees with desire and longing?

And he wouldn't have mentioned that he'd admitted to the wild chemical attraction. That wouldn't have pleased his large lady!

'I don't know what you mean,' she said stiltedly, watching James as the two men drew nearer, deliberately encasing her heart in ice because it was better to feel coldly, unrepentantly angry than full of hurt. She felt betrayed. She and James had shared something, if only the secret of their unwanted attraction. And he had taken her side of the secret—carefully omitting to mention his own—and given it to his fiancée as a joke, something to snigger about.

'I think you do,' Stephanie said, her voice low and hard. 'I don't blame you for fancying him. He's every woman's dream lover. But I do blame you for making it so obvious. He's mine, after all, so don't you forget it.' She had a smile on her face now, for James's benefit, of course, and as she took the glass of chilled white wine he'd brought her she slid along the bench seat and patted the vacant space. 'Sit by me, darling.'

Shoved up against the cast-iron arm rest, Zoe scrambled to her feet, her mind made up. She didn't need to plan a bunch of self-protective tactics because James had handed them to her on a plate. He thought she was an amoral tramp, had refused to allow her and Luke to stay behind in the empty villa, had clearly warned Paolo off. All because he couldn't bear to think of any other man taking what he believed she indiscriminately offered around!

At this precise moment she hated him with an intensity that fired her up on all cylinders, making it easy to do exactly what she had in mind.

Clutching her own glass of wine, she tucked her arm through Paolo's and mentally thanked him for the way his black eyes gleamed, the way his sensual mouth softened.

'You offered to give me a guided tour,' she reminded huskily. 'So why don't we leave the love-birds to it?'

'Delighted!' he quickly agreed, but his eyes widened, the glance he sent in James's direction incredulous. He was amazed because she had had the temerity to disobey a warning coming from the mighty Cade, Zoe translated, refusing to look at James. Just imagining that furious ice-grey stare was bad enough.

But he thoroughly deserved what he was about to get and she wasn't about to compromise her anger, her sense of betrayal, for any old-fashioned ideas about the way a properly brought up nice girl should behave.

She was going to make him squirm. She was going to make him burn!

She didn't have the slightest qualm when Paolo offered to show her over the house. While he had introduced her to some of his friends—most of whom, thankfully, spoke English—lingered a while around the pool then helped them to more wine at the buffet, she had realised with no small amount of relief that, like most blatantly flirtatious males he was all mouth and no trousers, happy to display a pretty girl on his arm but not knowing quite what to do about her.

And her tactics were working, she decided with grim satisfaction. Every time she looked up it was to find

James's hard grey eyes on her, his driven features displaying his cold, bitter anger.

He couldn't keep away. Even when he was apparently enjoying a casual conversation with various of the other guests—Stephanie glued to his side, as usual—he couldn't stop watching her with those hard empty eyes.

'I'd love to look around,' she agreed, wriggling a little closer in the circle of Paolo's proprietorial arm. 'If your mother won't mind,' she temporised, her spine prickling as she felt James's eyes boring into the back of her head.

'Of course not. And it will be cooler inside.' Paolo walked her up to the open main door and yes, it was much cooler inside, the thick stone walls keeping out the sultry heat.

A heavy door led to what Zoe took to be the main sitting-room. Colourful rugs softened the terracotta tiles of the floor and the furniture was dark wood, chunkily carved antiques, and Zoe made all the right admiring noises, thankful that her reading of his character had been correct. He made no attempt to touch her or make one of his outrageous suggestions. There was no one to overhear, no one to impress with his ability to appropriate the flaxen-haired foreigner.

When they reached the traditional farmhouse kitchen, all scrubbed pine, rush matting and copper cooking utensils, Paolo said ingenuously, 'Why did you say James and Stephanie were love-birds? From the way he was warning me off I thought you were his property. That I could understand.' He grinned disarmingly. 'The other I would have a great deal of difficulty with.'

There was no answer she could give. She could hardly say, He'd like to take me to bed but he can't because he's going to marry his chairman's daughter. So she simply shrugged, brushing her fingers lightly over the spice-scented petals of a potted geranium, dismissing, 'I'm not anyone's property. Do you think we should go back to the others? Won't your mother be wondering why you're not helping to entertain her guests?'

'Soon.' He took her dismissal of his question with good grace, telling her, 'You haven't seen upstairs yet.' And led the way up the service staircase, whisked her through a great many rooms then showed her what he had really wanted her to see all along.

Every available surface in his room was covered with Formula One memorabilia. And he turned to her, grinning, a bulky helmet held reverently in his hands.

'This was Fangio's. He wore it when he took the drivers' championship. And here...' Item by item, he displayed all his treasures, and Zoe decided she liked him very much indeed, especially when he confided, 'Since I was a little boy, I wanted to race. It took me until I was seventeen to understand that I had not the wealth, the connections or the talent. So I started collecting instead!'

'And have done it very thoroughly.' Zoe smiled at his enthusiasm. He was like an overgrown schoolboy, far removed from the image of the practised seducer he tried to project. She glanced at her watch. Her stomach was rumbling, grumbling because she'd missed out on breakfast. 'Shouldn't we go down?' she asked. 'I'm starving.' Even up here she could detect the delicious aromas of the barbecued food, and Paolo put a signed photograph of Stirling Moss back in its place, ruffled her hair, scattering the restraining pins, and acquiesced.

'Then I shall feed you. You shall have all the goodies you can eat, I promise.'

Zoe pushed at her mass of hair as she walked at his side down the wide main staircase. There had been nothing sexual in the way he'd pushed his hands through it, leaving it in such a mess. The gesture had been brotherly. She could imagine him doing it to Pilar, his handsome sister—and probably to his mother, too. A teasing gesture, used to reinforce his male superiority!

They had spent a long time in the house, almost an hour, but she had been glad of the respite. Flirting with Paolo, responding wholeheartedly to his casual touches and softly whispered innuendoes, constantly aware of the way James watched them both, particularly her, had wound her up to the point of near explosion, the adrenalin pumping through her blood at a thousand miles an hour.

So the quiet, friendly time spent with Paolo had relaxed her, or so she thought. Because when she saw James standing in the hall quite alone, watching them descend the stairs together, the rumpled wildness of her hair drawing his black brows together in a heavy scowl, the tension, as sharp and burning as a red-hot blade, came right back, making her flesh quiver.

Her instinct was to shrink back against the wall, to try to escape those searing eyes. But pride and a wicked need to retaliate had her continuing on down, unaware that Paolo was now lagging behind, a fixed smile on her lips and a voice in her head that screamed out, Yes, burn, you devil! Burn!

Perhaps now he would have some inkling of what she'd felt like when she'd watched Stephanie crawl all over him, when she'd lain awake at night wondering if he had gone to his fiancée's bed. Perhaps now he would understand what it felt like to want someone you knew you could never have so badly that it ripped you apart!

But something about the black pain that fleetingly appeared in his eyes made her heart clench inside her, made her put out a hand to steady herself against the wall, a mist in front of her eyes.

Then he turned on his heels and strode outside, and Paolo, trying to laugh but only succeeding in sounding anxious, said, 'I hope you were telling the truth when you said you weren't his property. He probably thinks we've spent the last hour in bed! I've only met him two or three times, and I don't mind standing up to him if there's a crowd around. But I wouldn't like to meet him alone in a dark alley if I'd got on the wrong side of the bastard!'

Given what he thought her track record was, the way she'd been playing up to Paolo, there was no 'probably' about it, Zoe thought with a sickening lurch of her heart, and followed the Portuguese man out through a side door that led to a shady green courtyard.

There were laughing, chattering groups of people sitting at tables, eating and drinking among the tubs of lemon trees, roses and geraniums.

'Find somewhere to sit,' Paolo suggested. 'I will fetch you something to eat.'

'It's OK.' Zoe did her best not to sound dejected, to let him know how affected she'd been by what she thought she had fleetingly seen in James's eyes. 'I'd rather choose for myself.'

She walked through the arch in the courtyard wall, and Paolo made no objections. He couldn't have failed to pick up the spearing tension between her and James just now and he had obviously decided that playing the lady-killer wasn't a bundle of laughs, after all.

The long buffet tables were groaning with delicious-looking food. Barbecued steaks and plump silver sardines, bowls of tiny new potatoes, salads, crispy breads and a wide selection of cheeses. But her appetite had left her and Zoe passed by, barely sparing the goodies a glance.

She had to be alone for a while, away from these friendly people who were all having a wonderful time. Away from James and his watchful eyes.

Until she and Paolo had disappeared inside the house she hadn't been able to escape him or the messages those silver eyes had conveyed. There had been brooding desire in the way he'd raked his glance over the slender naked length of her legs, the flare of her hips, the few inches of bare flesh above her tiny waist, the proud jut of her breasts where they were just confined in the cosseting soft fabric of her top. And hard, hurting dislike as she turned back to her chosen escort, her lips playing at smiling for him, her eyes pretending to tease.

Zoe shuddered, leaving the terraces, looking for the gate in the perimeter wall, which, so Paolo had told her earlier, opened on to the track that led down over the headland to the secluded cove he had talked about.

She had been playing a silly, demeaning game. Hurt pride, a sense of betrayal, all that love she was desperately trying to turn into hate making her behave recklessly. Making her ashamed of herself.

The grassy track was well-defined, the scent of wild herbs sharp and astringent in the heavy air, and perhaps, down on the shore, there would be a breeze from the sea to temper the oppression that was making her shorts and halter top cling damply to her body, her hair a heavy weight on the nape of her neck.

Five minutes later her hopes were dashed. There wasn't a hint of a breeze to stir the air and the sea looked like glass, barely moving as it sluggishly lapped the shoreline.

But, no matter, at least she had the place to herself, space around her, a little time at her disposal to get herself back together.

The black look of pain she had briefly glimpsed in James's eyes as she and Paolo had descended those stairs together had shaken her to the depths of her soul. She had deliberately set out to hurt him, to torture him the way seeing him with Stephanie had tortured her.

And, so it seemed, she had succeeded. But it brought no triumph. Only pain. She didn't want to hurt him. His pain was her pain; that was what loving meant. She had learned a lesson she wouldn't forget in a hurry, she thought, scuffing her feet in the sand. And she was going to have to work out how she would get through the remainder of her time in Portugal. With her teeth permanently gritted, she supposed. Because there would be absolutely no point at all in facing James and apologising for her stupid antics. The way she had behaved would only have reinforced his scathing opinion of her and might actually have served to extinguish the unwilling physical attraction he'd felt for her.

Well, so be it. Her love for him wasn't going anywhere. It had never stood a chance. Sex was all he had wanted from her and such was his self-discipline, his implacability, that he had been able to ignore it, put it aside, marking it down as a minor irritation that would fade away if he willed it to do so.

Which was just as well, she recognised bleakly. Because even if all those moral principles she embraced sternly told her that sex without love and deep commitment on both sides was demeaning and not for her, she knew, with painful honesty, that she wouldn't have had the will to deny him if he had decided to take her to his bed and take what he wanted, scratching the itch instead of ignoring it until it went away.

So she had to be grateful for his self-control. The taste of heaven he would have given her would have soon become soured when she faced the fact that he had used her as a one-night stand, viewing her with the contempt she would have deserved.

A rumble of thunder growled through the distant hills, and then another, sounding closer. Zoe sighed, lifting her hands to push the weight of her hair up away from her neck. She would have to make her way back to the party. When the storm broke the guests would all take shelter in the house or beneath the awning. And the party would break up. The thought of the drive back to the villa with James and the others made her feel ill. But it had to be faced.

She turned, making her way back to the head of the cove, and stopped dead. Frozen to stone. He was standing at the end of the track, just above the sand. Watching her.

Her pulses raced and the ground no longer felt solid beneath her feet. Wave after wave of need and longing swept through her, making her shudder. And her breath clogged in her throat, making her heart race.

How long had he been there, watching, waiting? Had he decided it was time to leave, come to fetch her because someone had seen her come this way? It seemed the only possible explanation.

A sudden squall of wind came with an ominously close clap of thunder, forcing her to make her reluctant legs move over the sand. He was as still as one of the obelisks that were found along the coast, as deep in mystery. She shuddered and fought for control. She must not think like that. The only reason for his being here at all was to hurry her back because he was ready to leave. No mystery in that, she told herself staunchly, and made herself hurry because the first heavy drops of rain were falling, threatening a deluge.

She had known she would have to face him sooner or later, see the contempt for her earlier behaviour deep in those compelling silver eyes. That she would rather it had been later, in the company of others was, she supposed, just punishment for her foolishness.

Tightening her mouth, she pushed on, came closer, close enough to see the eyes in that expressionless face. She flinched, lowered her eyes to the ground in front of her feet. Not contempt. Retribution.

'I'm sorry you had to come all this way to fetch me.' She knew her only salvation lay in acting normally, if she was not to bring his scorn crashing down around her head. But her wretched voice sounded ragged, and she did her best to control her breathing as she sidestepped him. 'We'll have to make a run for it or we'll get drenched.'

'No.' An arm snaked out around her neck, dragging her, feet skidding on the wet grass, hard against his body. His voice was tight as he bit out the single word, as if he were holding a volcano of emotions in check, refusing—just—to let them erupt.

The rain was soaking his shirt, moulding it even closer to his body, soaking his hair, small rivulets running down the hard, driven features. And, so close to him, his body heat seared her, the grim line of his mouth above that hard, implacable jaw drawing her like a weak and feeble moth to the flame of his scorching masculinity.

Zoe began to tremble. She was shaking so much she could barely speak, but managed rawly, 'Let me go!'

'Give me one good reason why I should,' he demanded savagely, his hands coming up on either side of her head, her wet blonde hair snaking between his fingers. 'You know how much I ache to possess your wicked little body. Why should I deny myself what others are allowed to take freely?'

Something sharp and terrifying twisted deep inside her, leaving her barely able to stand, forcing her to clutch on to his sinewy forearms for support. And she heard his ragged intake of air as her fingers dug into hard muscle and bone and she forced out on a tiny sob, 'You don't mean that!'

But he did mean it, every bitter word. There was a wildness in his eyes, turning them black, a white shade around his mouth. She had tormented him beyond endurance and there was punishment written deeply in his eyes, scored across his ravaged features.

'Try me!' His teeth snapped. 'And don't tell me you're not eager for it again!' There was a cynical curl to his hard mouth as his hands slid down to her shoulders to grip tightly, holding her upper body away. 'I can read the physical signs as well as any man.' His eyes raked the full globes of her breasts, fastening on the twin points of arousal, clearly visible through the fine wet fabric. Shame rolled round inside her, dragging her down, and she heard his voice as if it came from a great distance away. 'What happened? Didn't young Paolo live up to expectations? Or are you insatiable, like a bitch on permanent heat?'

Her head fell forward on her slender neck, the wet curtain of her hair hiding her anguished face. She had to tell him the truth, about her feelings for him, the way she'd tormented him, deliberately flirted with Paolo to pay him back. But how could she? She couldn't find the words.

Twisting her hair around his wrist like a rope, he drew her head back. The sky had darkened dramatically with the downpour but she could see the glitter of his eyes as he told her, 'Look at me when I speak. Let me read the lie in your eyes when you tell me you don't want me to make love to you to within an inch of your life right here and now. Try to tell me you're not burning for me as much as I'm burning for you and I'll say you're a liar.'

His feet planted firmly apart, the force of his arousal branded her through the sodden barrier of their clothing as slowly, deliberately, he used one hand to unfasten her halter top, letting the material fall to the ground, before he circled one engorged nipple and then the other with his forefinger, still watching her with an intensity that scarred her soul.

Then, just as deliberately, he turned his hand, cupping his long, supple fingers beneath her breast, sending shock-waves of aching desire through her body, shock-waves that faded into insignificance as he lowered his dark head to suckle.

The ecstasy was unbearable, beyond her wildest imaginings, the tumult inside her putting the storm to shame. She had longed for his touch until the very thought of him had become an obsession. But not like this. Never like this!

Gathering the little strength still remaining in her trembling limbs, she tried to twist away, beating at his body with her small open hands. But he captured both of them easily with one of his own, his pupils dilated, black with scorn and an unstoppable sob of hopeless despair boiled up inside her and broke until she was weeping with an intensity that pulled her apart.

Struggling for self-control, she felt his body go very still, and her tears mingled with the rain, drowning her features with misery and, for a timeless moment, tension beat between them until he dragged her into his arms with a groan and covered her tears with his mouth, each and every one of them, and she subsided against him weakly, clinging to him because, apart from the time she had cut her lip, this was the first tenderness he'd shown her and this was what she had yearned for, above and beyond the driving physical need.

His hands were softly soothing the naked skin of her back; warm, sliding hands, making magic against her rain-slicked flesh. And his mouth at last found the corner of hers, paused for a tiny, fraught second and then moved on, slowly, sensually exploring the full ripe curves. And this was the wonderful, the instinctive continuation of tenderness, the magical explosion of desire.

Parting her eager lips, she felt the sudden, savage hunger as his kiss deepened, and twined her arms around his neck, her body pressed willingly down the length of his. A sense of fatality numbed her mind as she gloried in sensations that were utterly new to her.

Nothing could stop what was about to happen. It was written, pre-ordained. Nothing existed but their mutual, terrible and tumultuous need, this deep, primeval passion.

'Zoe!' Her name was torn from him as he lifted his mouth from hers and stared blindly into her eyes and as she slid small eager hands beneath the hem of his T-shirt, his nostrils flared and he dragged in a ragged breath. 'God, Zoe, I want you, need you!' He lowered his head, raining urgent kisses against her neck, ranging

down over her breasts, her taut midriff, dealing sum-
marily with the button on the waistband of her shorts,
sloughing them down the long, elegant line of her legs
until she was naked, gloriously unashamed, eager to give
him all she had to offer.

Slowly, his eyes ate every inch of her body and then
locked with hers. And she saw the dark torment and
held out her arms to him because for her the torment
was over, glorious certainty taking its place. She wanted
it to be the same for him, she needed it to be the same
for him, and made a feral sound deep in her throat as
triumph glittered silver in his eyes and he crushed her
to him, cradling her in his arms as they subsided on to
the soft damp grass. And this was her world, he was her
world; she had entered a different plane, a place where
no one came, where only she and the man she loved
existed. Time was no longer measured in minutes, but
in the ecstatic exploration of hands and lips and eyes,
in the tumult of flesh against flesh, skin against skin, in
the perfect counterpoint of hard male dominance and
silky feminine softness.

And when he entered her at last her heart sang with
the lyrical loveliness of finally coming home, of sharing
this dance of ecstasy with the man who ruled her heart,
her mind, her senses. But as he encountered the tightness
of her virginal barrier she felt him go very still, and the
world stopped breathing until he rolled away from her,
his head in his hands, and she cried out in a drowning
voice, 'James—don't! Don't leave me now! Oh, James—
I love you—I love you so!'

She saw the bones of his wide shoulders lock as her
anguish shivered through the air and she scrambled to
her knees, imploring, 'Tell me why, tell me
what's wrong!'

He lifted his head and began, slowly, reluctantly, to turn towards her and then went very still, his sudden, violent expletive punching the silence, shocking her, until, following the fixed direction of his gaze she saw a still figure on the track above them.

Although it had stopped raining and the sun was breaking through the melting clouds, the man above them was holding a scarlet umbrella above his head. It looked surreal, like a bloated exclamation mark and, even as her horrified eyes registered all this, the stranger turned, closed the umbrella, used it as a walking stick as he made his way back up the track.

Her face flaming with embarrassment, Zoe scrambled into her clothes, the sodden fabric feeling horrible against her skin. But not nearly as horrible as she felt inside. And James, too, must be disgusted. Had some sixth sense alerted him to the man's presence? Had he stopped making love to her because he'd sensed they were being watched?

Somehow, in all this awful mess, that made her feel a little better and she turned to him, tears trembling on her lashes.

'I hate Peeping Toms!'

He closed the zip of his jeans with a metallic rasp, his eyes grim.

'It's a public place. And that's no Peeping Tom. That was Patrick Wright. My chairman.'

CHAPTER ELEVEN

ZOE tucked the little boys in bed, dropped loving kisses on flushed cheeks and watched two pairs of bright eyes droop with sleep before she walked softly out of the room.

A great hard lump of pain settled beneath her breastbone as, her mouth compressed, she went quickly down the stairs and out into the warm early August evening and sat on the doorstep, battling with emotions that were proving impossible to control.

There had been a few times when she'd congratulated herself that she'd been well on the way to getting her life together again. She'd returned from Portugal with a frantic determination to forget James Cade and all that had happened, throwing herself into her work, finding an apartment more convenient for her office, moving out of the basement she shared with Jenna, who was still pondering whether to move in with Henry. Moving in with her family, taking a week's leave while she waited for the furnishings she'd chosen to be delivered to the apartment.

But no matter how hectic, her life still contained those moments when black grief engulfed her, and instead of getting fewer they were becoming more frequent.

She couldn't forget James, couldn't stop loving him. In fact, she loved him more, now that she knew why he was the way he was. He was always there, haunting her, slipping past her guard and into her mind.

The drive back to the villa after Claudia's fateful party was a dark stain on her memory. James had been silent and withdrawn, not bothering to respond to Stephanie's increasingly huffy remarks until, eventually, she had fallen silent too, staring out of the window, her lower lip jutting mutinously like a child's. And, after giving her still damp and rumpled appearance a quizzical stare, Luke had lain his head back on the leather upholstery and slept for the duration of the journey.

Mercifully, Patrick Wright was staying on at the farmhouse. It was the only consolation Zoe had. As he and Claudia had seen them off he'd told his daughter to expect him at the villa some time the next day. Claudia had had her arm hooked through his, a big smile on her face because he had changed his mind and made time to be with her on her birthday. Zoe had felt too ill with embarrassment to look at him.

She'd spent what was left of the evening in her room and in the morning James had gone.

'Caught a flight back to London at some godforsaken hour,' Luke told her as he intercepted her on her way to the kitchen in search of strong black coffee, which was all the breakfast she'd been able to stomach that morning. 'He said to see you got this.' He held out the briefcase James had confiscated, and, raising a brow, remarked drily, 'Armour back in place, I see!' Meaning the neat navy blue skirt she was wearing with a crisp white shirt, of course, and she shrugged, not interested in his opinions, only interested in containing the sudden rush of tears that clogged her throat.

James had gone and she didn't need to be a fortuneteller to know he wouldn't be back. Not while she was here. No messages, just the briefcase. She had opened her heart to him, blurted out her love for him. Surely, if he had a heart at all, he would have spared her a soft word of regret? Something!

Perhaps his prospective father-in-law had ordered him to go, Zoe thought chokily. A man who could openly betray his precious daughter with another woman would be given short shrift. She didn't want him to marry the ghastly woman but she didn't want him to travel through life hating her for wrecking his careful plans. Because he would blame her for what had happened, and perhaps with justification. He had had his side of the wild mutual attraction under strict control until she had tormented him with Paolo.

'Are you sickening for something?' Luke asked, his eyes astute as he pushed his hands into the pockets of his crisp white shorts. 'Or did something happen yesterday I ought to know about? James also looked like death last night when he told me he was leaving and gave me your case.'

'Did he?' She affected indifference. 'No, I'm not sickening.' She ignored the other question. 'Too much wine yesterday,' she lied briskly, patting the briefcase as she suggested, 'Now I've got my hands on this, we can go through it together. It is what you're supposed to be here to do, isn't it?'

She'd had to emerge for lunch; she couldn't hide forever. And, to her mortified horror, Patrick Wright was there. It had been as much as she could do to choke down one forkful of food, even though he'd treated her with polite friendliness. Nothing to betray that he'd watched her making love with his prospective son-in-law. And Stephanie was acting normally. If her father had told her what he'd seen she would have scratched her eyes out long ago.

Which probably meant that Patrick was willing to turn a blind eye. Men stuck together over that sort of thing. He probably didn't want to lose the best chief executive he was ever likely to have. And James had undoubtedly passed the whole regrettable incident off as a fling with a baggage who'd been begging for it—nothing important. Lots of men would have understood that approach, and many would actually condone it. Patrick Wright was obviously one of those!

Zoe stopped pushing her salad around her plate, laid her fork down and said, 'If you'll excuse me, I'll get back to my work,' and had almost reached the door of her room when a soft voice halted her.

'May I have a moment of your time, my dear?'

Zoe cringed. This was it, then. He was going to ask her to leave, too. Perhaps he had ordered James off his premises, was waiting until she had left before breaking the news of what he had seen to his daughter. Shakily, she turned to face the chairman of Wright and Grantham, expecting cold contempt and finding instead a curious blend of wariness and sympathy on his craggy face.

'You'll probably say this is none of my business but I think I should warn you, you're playing with fire. I've known James many years. I admire and respect him and openly admit that, though I might be titular head of the company, James is the brain behind its success. He's like a son to me, but I have no illusions. If you allow your affair with him to continue you'll be storing up grief.'

Zoe gaped at him, her throat going dry. He was warning her off. He would probably do anything to prevent his daughter hearing about her fiancé's supposed affair with the book-keeper woman!

She shuddered inside and said thickly, 'You don't understand. What—what happened wasn't James's fault.' It took a lot out of her to remind the elderly man verbally of what he had seen, to shoulder the blame. But the responsibility had been hers——

'Of course it was his fault,' Patrick argued drily. He glanced at the elegant two-seater sofa placed against the wall of the spacious corridor. 'I think we should sit down.'

Zoe had little choice but to fall in with the suggestion. Suddenly, her legs seemed to have turned to water.

Patrick said kindly, 'You're upset. I'm sorry, but I felt I had to say something. You've only been here a week; you can't have become too emotionally embroiled.' He gave her an encouraging smile, but his grey eyes were sombre. 'I've never interfered in his private life before. He's not a womaniser, far from it, but there have been women. Two, to my knowledge. Short-term mistresses chosen with wisdom and discretion. Women capable of accepting dismissal when the time came. Glossy, sophisticated creatures with hearts firmly in the deep freeze. I only had to note the way you couldn't look me in the eye after I'd unwittingly stumbled across the two of you yesterday, the way you blushed and trembled and tried to hide it, the way your face was so tired and strained while you tried to act naturally and pretended to eat your lunch, to know you were completely different from the other two. I know you won't thank me for it, but I had to warn you. If you start believing James will say he loves you, start dreaming of a wedding-ring and happily-ever-after, you're going to be badly hurt.'

She lifted unhappy green eyes to his. How could she tell this kindly man—who seemed genuinely concerned—that she had no illusions on that score? That far from returning her love, he probably hated her, blamed her for his loss of control. That marriage to his daughter was his object because of who he, Patrick, was!

'What happened was madness,' she assured him instead, her voice thick with suppressed emotion. 'It won't happen again and I won't let myself be hurt.' She tried to smile to bolster the lie, but it didn't quite come off. Of course she was hurting and his wry smile told her he knew it, but it was the best she could do.

'You're a fighter,' he approved gently. 'That helps. And don't blame yourself. As long as you understand that James is psychologically unable to make an emotional commitment to any woman, you'll cope. What his mother was is no secret. What James does keep hidden is the way she was responsible for his inability to trust or respect or love any woman.'

Giving her arm a brief consoling pat, he left her. Left her staring into space, forlornly putting two and two together. Perhaps she needn't have been so sensitive about mentioning his daughter's forthcoming marriage to James. Patrick had acknowledged that he knew of his future son-in-law's affairs, his inability to love. So maybe the three of them were open about the engagement—accepting it for what it would culminate in— a marriage of convenience.

The chairman of Wright and Grantham hadn't been warning her off because he saw her as a threat to his daughter's happiness, but because he was a decent man and she, as he had said, was different from the short-term mistresses he knew about. Added to which, she was working for his company, a guest at his villa. He felt responsible.

So she'd sorted out why Patrick hadn't told her to pack her bags, that he accepted the marriage of convenience idea and would turn a blind eye to James's future affairs provided they were conducted with the discretion and wisdom he'd talked about. But it didn't make her feel any better. Worse, if anything, because how could she have lost her head and fallen deeply and hopelessly in love with a man who didn't know the meaning of the word?

And what did his mother have to do with the way he was? It was a question that gnawed at her brain over the next few days. To begin with he'd tightened up dramatically whenever she'd mentioned his family and then, later, he had volunteered information about his father, his respect and affection for his parent coming over strongly. But barely a word about his mother. Simply the fact that her father had met her when he was a very young man and had married her because a child was on the way.

But that couldn't have traumatised him, surely? It was too ridiculous to think about. Granted, his father had found himself in straitened circumstances, had had to forget his ambition to teach. But he had eventually done well out of the mundane job he had been forced to take.

Loving him as she did, she wanted to know what had gone wrong between him and his mother, leaving him emotionally barren. She wanted to understand. Knowing why he was the way he was might help to ease the pain of loving him.

It wasn't until the night before Luke was due to return to England that Zoe found an opportunity to ask. Patrick had said that what his mother had been was no secret, so maybe Luke could enlighten her.

Patrick and Stephanie were dining with Claudia and Zoe tapped on Luke's door and walked in.

He was packing in a desultory fashion and he said, 'I'm sorry to be leaving, but I can't justify another day. I bet it's raining in London.'

'Sure to be!' She grinned at his doleful expression, then sobered. She wished she were going with him. But work would keep her here for another couple of days at least. She couldn't wait to go; there were too many painful memories.

She sat on the edge of the bed, watching him ram the last of his things into his case, and she asked quickly, before she lost her courage, 'Do you know anything about James Cade's mother?' and didn't understand why he looked up from what he was doing, plastered a spuriously pious look on his face and said with faked outrage,

'Me? A respectable married man?'

'No, seriously!' She frowned at him, shaking her head and his eyes widened. Then he fastened his case and straightened up.

'You mean you don't know?'

'Should I?'

He stared at her for a second then reasoned, 'Probably not. Her death made the headlines ten years ago; you'd have been too young to take any interest in the articles that proliferated over the subsequent few weeks. Besides, all good parents would have hidden the newspapers from young and impressionable kids! It must have been agony for Cade, but he was clever enough not to deny the relationship. If it was out in the open he wouldn't have any nasty skeletons in the cupboard for unscrupulous people to winkle out. His father had died a couple of months earlier, so at least he was spared that kind of embarrassment.'

'You're not making a whole lot of sense,' Zoe pointed out, puzzled and beginning to get impatient. 'She must have been someone well-known to have articles written about her.'

'Oh, very—in certain quarters.' He joined her on the bed, swinging his feet up and leaning back against the headboard. 'Extremely well-known by certain peers of the realm, cabinet ministers, senior civil-servants! Caroline Cade, my dear little innocent, was a madam. She kept what is commonly known as a knocking shop.'

Zoe gasped at his crudity, her heart banging like a drum. Poor James! His attitudes began to make sense. She twisted her hands together in her lap, her eyes distressed as Luke elaborated.

'There was nothing common about her establishment, though. According to those articles she was very discreet, very expensive. The girls she employed were all carefully vetted—mostly out of the top drawer of society, sophisticated, able to keep their mouths shut about what they did for a living. And what a living! Caroline Cade died a wealthy woman. Everything was left to James, who promptly donated every penny to charity. Trouble was, she wasn't discreet about her dying! Admittedly, she didn't plan it. The Kensington house went up in flames. Arson? An outraged wife? Nobody ever knew. Caroline was the only one to die, but the fire officers pulled a few well-known and very red faces out of that inferno. The tabloids had a field day, of course. Dug up everything they could find about her past—the fact that she'd married when she was seventeen, had had a son who was going places in the world of big business. I could go on, but I think you get the picture.'

And indeed she had, Zoe thought now, getting up from the step, flexing her stiff limbs and brushing off the well-worn jeans she was wearing. She understood many things about him now. The stiff lecture he'd given her that night when he'd thought she was a fifteen-year-old hooker. His disgust at what he thought were her lax morals, the difficulty he had in believing in her integrity—the list was endless, and, far from easing the pain of loving him, the insight she'd been given had only made her love deepen.

She sighed heavily with exasperation and pushed her long blonde hair back off her face. She had this increasing tendency to sit and brood about James whenever she had an idle moment. It had to stop. In future, idle moments would not be allowed!

There were still a couple of hours of daylight left and the hedge at the side of her father's cottage needed clipping. She would hear if either of the twins woke because their bedroom window was just above where she was working, and it wasn't likely that they would because Petra and Phil had had them out all day, taking a picnic. They had been healthily tired out when Petra had left with Phil at six this evening.

Things seemed to be going smoothly with those two, Zoe thought, determined not to let James get a foothold in her mind. Phil was a kind, caring man with a great sense of humour—just what Petra needed. And he was good with the twins, accepting them readily with no sign of the resentment a lesser man would have shown. And this evening he had taken Petra to meet his parents, and that was a good sign, she approved, clipping away as if her life depended on it.

And Dad and Barbara Evans were getting on famously, she told herself, furious because her treacherous mind had started wondering what James was doing now, where he was, whether the wedding-date had been fixed yet.

So yes, it looked as though her father might have found a companion to partner him through the rest of his life. He had, so Petra had confided, asked Barbara to choose colour schemes for the cottage. The whole place needed redecorating, new curtains, too, and it was her advice he'd asked for, not his daughters', and they'd spent long happy hours together poring over samples of paints, wallpapers and fabrics. And tonight he'd taken her out to dinner—a regular Sunday evening occurrence, apparently—and—— Oh, it was no use! No matter how hard she tried to think of other things, she couldn't keep James out of her head!

A sob built up inside her. She felt as if she'd swallowed a brick. And then, unstoppably, the release of the tears which were far too ready these days. Angrily, she scrubbed them away, transferring great smudges of dust from the privet hedge to her small triangular face.

Love hurt. It hurt like hell! It could do dreadful things to you. She had been so right to be wary of it, to steer herself carefully away from any hint of it. And so feebly, wilfully foolish to let herself fall fathoms deep in love with a man who, for his own troubled reasons, couldn't love her back. Couldn't love anyone.

Through the storm of her angry misery she heard the sound of a car coming up the lane. Pulling herself together, she picked up the abandoned shears and relaunched her attack on the hedge. It could be someone from the village, or a casual passer-by, out for an evening country drive. Whoever—she didn't want anyone to see her in this state.

The engine stopped. Directly outside the gate, she guessed. Probably someone asking for directions, she muttered inside her head and carried on snipping, hoping the driver had merely stopped to consult a map. But her run of bad luck was still striding along, she accepted resignedly as she heard the wicket gate creak on its hinges, purposeful footsteps advancing along the path.

Knowing she must look a pitiful fright, with her eyes all puffy and red from weeping, streaky cheeks and mussed up hair, she turned reluctantly and the world tipped upside-down and exploded around her.

For a moment she thought she was going to faint but was held, almost against her will, by the forceful glitter of James's silver eyes. Like a coward, she would have preferred the oblivion of unconsciousness, anything rather than have to see him again, see those well-loved imperious features, the lithe grace of his body so perfectly packaged in a beautifully cut dark business suit.

Seeing him, so close yet so impossibly distant, stirred up the dark and fatal fascination she was fighting so hard to forget. She didn't know what had brought him here and decided, apathetically, that the way her luck was running it couldn't be good.

She lowered her eyes miserably. She was shaking inside and trying not to let it show. She didn't know how to handle this and flinched violently when he put out a hand and touched the side of her face.

'You've been crying. Why?' The deep, gravelly voice was inexpressibly tender, yet threaded through with a tension she couldn't understand.

Everything inside her dissolved, fragmented. His tenderness had been her undoing before, she remembered, and fought it, telling him toughly, 'No reason. Just tired. What are you doing here?'

'You don't cry because you're tired. You're tougher than that.' A trace of the old mocking arrogance in his voice had her chin jutting up and his hand fell back to his side as he added, 'I'm here to see you. I can't think of any other reason, can you? I phoned Halraike Hopkins and Luke told me you were on leave, staying with your father.'

'I see,' she said tightly, her mind moving out of shock. Business. What else? Had she fouled up? Probably, the state she'd been in during those final few days in Portugal. 'Shall we go inside?' Her voice didn't sound like her own at all and when she moved she felt like a very old woman. She didn't want to invite him in, yet what else could she do? They could hardly conduct a business discussion knee-deep in privet cuttings.

He followed her wordlessly, but she could feel his eyes eating into her back. It made her spine prickle. And she remembered that other time, when he had hardly taken his eyes off her at all—except when she'd disappeared with Paolo. She'd set out to tease, to pay him back, daring him to believe the worst of her. The memory made her feel ill.

'Make yourself comfortable.' She gestured stiltedly around the cluttered sitting-room. 'I'll make coffee.' And make time to wash her face, brush her hair, pin it back, give herself a much-needed breathing space.

But he took her arm, turning her round, his hand burning bare flesh below the old short-sleeved blouse she was wearing with her scruffy old jeans.

'I don't want coffee. I want to talk to you.'

She stared at the taut lines of his face and the floor shook beneath her feet. Was she to be allowed no respite at all? Not even a few desperately needed minutes? And he must have read the unspoken anguish in her eyes because he dragged her into his arms and groaned roughly.

'Don't look like that! It's too much punishment. I know how much I hurt you!'

She could hear the heavy beat of his heart, feel the warmth of him as her head was cradled against the front of his crisp white shirt, smell the subtle maleness of him—heady aphrodisiacs all—and she weakly allowed herself just a tiny moment of shuddering ecstasy before she pushed herself out of that particular fool's paradise.

He was obviously referring to her blundering, blurted confession of love and was sorry for her. And when he'd left without saying a word to her she'd mentally accused him of having no heart. She now knew he had, and wished he hadn't, wished he'd leave it, forget it.

'I know I'm handling this badly.' He watched her totter about the room, trying to look competent as she tidied the twins' toys away. 'I've bungled everything right from the beginning. I could kick myself. You probably despise me—you've every right. But will you let me try?'

He sounded hesitant, strangely diffident and she paused in her domestic flutterings to give him a wide-eyed stare. Diffident? The mighty Cade?

'Try what?' She did not believe that hesitancy. She could not believe it! Was this to be some twisted joke at her expense? A twist of the knife in an open wound? She gave him what she hoped would pass for a haughty glare, plucked a plastic car from the top of the television set and tossed it into the toy box.

And heard his impatient intake of breath and knew there wasn't a trace of diffidence to be found as he rapped out, 'Stop flapping around, Zoe!' He covered the carpet in two long strides and lifted her off her feet, depositing her at one end of the sofa while he took the other. 'We're alone, I take it?' He glanced round the room, as if expecting to see all the members of her family peering round the furniture. She nodded, too breathless to speak. 'You're baby-sitting, and they're asleep.' He didn't wait for an affirmative, took it as read, and then said softly, 'You've got a dirty face. You don't look more than a child yourself,' and that ruined whatever hope she'd had of getting her breath back and her recovery was even further delayed when he took both her hands in his and told her, 'I've always had to fight what you do to me. Fight the attraction that had me yearning to possess you—own you. I told you how you intrigued me—it was the mixture, as I perceived it, of saint and sinner. I never knew which one of you was real. My brain said "sinner" but my heart told me the sinner was sweet. It was the sweetness, the sensuality, all mixed up with prim efficiency that I couldn't handle. I told myself I could, of course. Then finally knew I couldn't when I saw you allow Paolo to monopolise you, spirit you away——'

'Nothing happened,' she assured him shakily. He was going to apologise for what had happened on the headland. She couldn't bear that. She didn't want him to be sorry for losing control, to be deeply regretting those moments of rare and true ecstasy she'd found in his arms.

But he said grimly, 'Do you think I don't know that, now? When I discovered you were a virgin everything inside me exploded. For the first time in my life I didn't know how to cope. And so I took myself away and did some hard thinking.' His fingers tightened around her small hands and she didn't protest because the tiny pain was a gift. 'My heart was OK,' he said, his mouth twisting wryly. 'It knew what I wanted. It was my head that got in a mess. My heart knew I wanted you, had been falling more and more in love with you with each day that passed. But my head kept stepping in and saying my heart lied.' His eyes darkened suddenly. 'Do you

know anything about my background, other than wha
I've told you?'

She nodded, her heart aching for him. 'Luke told me
about—about your mother. He wasn't gossiping,' she
assured him quickly. 'I asked. Patrick had said some
thing about her—said there was no secret about it. I had
to know all I could about you. I needed to!'

'Yes,' he said, as if he understood that. His face wa
more sombre than she had ever seen it and she knew
bleakly, that he had done his thinking and believed hi
head, and not his heart, that the moment of soaring
blind happiness she'd grasped at when he'd confessed to
falling in love with her was the last she'd ever have.

Why else would he bring up the troubled subject o
his mother if it weren't to explain that discovering wha
she was, after her death, had so traumatised him tha
he was incapable of loving or trusting any woman?

'I understand,' she said with gentle compassion. 'I
would have come as a terrible shock to read those article
after her death.'

Still grasping her captured hands, he impressed, '
knew what my mother was long before then. Dad told
me when I was eighteen. What shocked me—really
shocked me—was learning she'd paid the huge fees fo
my schooling. It was the first and last time I ever ver
bally fought with my father. Oh, as I grew older I'
wondered how such an expensive education could b
afforded. Dad was earning a reasonably comfortabl
living wage by that time, but nothing beyond that. Whe
I asked him he gave vague answers about grant system
and, with the ignorance of youth, I believed him. He'
lied to me, and that hurt. That he'd taken anything from
her shocked me. He told me how my mother's con
science made her offer the money, that he'd never ac

cepted a penny except the school fees, and had only agreed to that because he believed that she owed me something and that the best reparation she could make was the finest education available.'

'Did you ever see her?' Zoe questioned, a slow burn of anger building up in her heart for the woman who had made this man incapable of respecting her sex. Gradually, she released her fingers from his punitive grip and slid them gently over the backs of his hands. The small, soothing gesture seemed to relax him, because he answered more lightly.

'On a few occasions, yes. Sometimes she'd take me out at half-term—a visit to the zoo, tea at some grand hotel, lunch when I grew older. She always seemed like a stranger, but then she would, wouldn't she? She walked out on me and my father when I was a few months old. There was a divorce. The first time I saw her was when I was twelve years old. I never thought to question why my father got custody—usually it goes the other way, especially when it means the child has to be left with a series of obliging neighbours each day. She was beautiful to look at. I remember thinking she was a mother any boy could be proud of. Beautifully dressed, very serene and, strangely, rather prim. I was at the age to be impressed, overawed. I couldn't understand why my father had ever let her go. And when he told me the truth I hated her, the façade she'd presented for my benefit disgusted me. Everything about her disgusted me! I knew I would never be able to trust another woman again,' he finished grimly.

'And you never saw her again?' Zoe asked, her voice threaded with sadness because he had just confirmed that those fleeting hopes had been stillborn.

'No,' he affirmed harshly. 'I refused to allow Dad to
accept anything more towards my education, put myself
through university, bolstering my grant by doing any
casual job that came my way. And forgot her. Until her
death in that fire, followed by a few resignations from
positions of high authority and those scurrilous article
in the tabloids. That brought it all right out in the open,
the whole sordid mess.'

And hardened his resolve to distrust all women, Zoe
thought miserably, not blaming him yet wishing with all
her heart that it could be different. It was growing dark
in the little room, the shadows sombre, echoing her
mood, and she reached over to flick on the table-lamp
at the side of the sofa and the gentle glow was playing
tricks because the hardness had gone from his face
revealing something she couldn't put a name to.

'I came back to England to get my head straightened
out,' he told her softly. 'And in doing that, could forgive
her. She had a tough start. Her own mother was sixteen
when she had her, and even at that tender age was unable
to name the father. Her schooling was patchy, she had
no one to care about her and when Dad fell in love with
her I don't think she knew how to handle it; she married
him because it gave her a kind of security, and left almost
as soon as I was born. She wanted more from life than
the grinding poverty she'd been brought up in—and Dad
was unable to offer her much more at that time. She
had a good brain, but no education to speak of. So she
used her body. And that, my darling Zoe, is the last time
we need to speak about her. In discovering the ability
to forgive I also discovered a greater truth.' He took a
unsteady breath. 'You said you loved me and I believed
you—that was the breakthrough. And I think you still
do, my darling. Will you answer one question?' Again

the slight pause, as if everything hinged on her answer. 'Will you let me love you?'

She shuddered, rocked to her soul. Be his mistress? Stay quietly in the background while he got on with his sham of a marriage, there for him when he wanted to slake all that wild and wonderful passion?

'No,' she said with rough anguish, saw his face go bleak, felt his hands slide away from hers. She looked down at her fingers. 'I won't be your mistress. It would kill me. Knowing Stephanie had first claim, waiting for your first child to be born, wondering when you would tell me goodbye because being a father gave you new moral responsibilities—I couldn't bear it, James!'

She could have said more, given a thousand reasons why she couldn't put herself through that kind of hell, but he pulled her into his arms, smothering her face with kisses, only drawing away to tell her, 'I don't want a mistress, only a wife. You. I will only ever want you, my darling. Marry me, quickly. Let me love you. Love, cherish and adore you.'

She gasped, delirious for the first time in her life, her head arching back as his plundering mouth found the underside of her jaw and began a slow, erotically tormenting descent down the slender stalk of her neck.

'You're going to have to choose somewhere for us to live. A bachelor flat's not the place for the most exquisite bride a man could ever have. Choose anything, anywhere. I'll tag along to make sure there's at least one bedroom big enough to take a large four-poster, with drapes we can use to close the whole world out...'

All the time he was seducing her with words he was seducing her with his lips. They were making dangerous forays between her breasts and somehow the buttons of her blouse had come adrift and things were rapidly getting out of hand, and before they did she had to know.

'Have you told Stephanie the engagement's off?'

'What engagement?' His lips moved to one side, discovering she hadn't bothered to wear her bra. Zoe gave his thick dark hair an impatient tug.

'Don't act dumb! You know very well. You were going to marry your chairman's daughter. You told me!' Her accusation was rendered feeble by her gasp of ecstasy as he found one nipple and tugged at it wickedly.

'No, I didn't.' He sighed, lifting his head. 'You're breaking my concentration! I said, if you remember, that it had been mentioned. Which it had. By her. Turned down flat. By me. She thought it was a splendid idea and, because her father is who he is, believed I'd jump at the opportunity. Her head's as big as the rest of her! I only let you think I was spoken for as a defence. I was still fighting what I felt for you. Now I'm not.'

Just to prove it, he kissed her thoroughly and when she could speak again she said giddily, 'But Stephanie told me herself——'

He laid a silencing finger against her mouth. 'Well she would, wouldn't she? I'd recently turned her down, kindly, I hope, but she was still feeling sore. And she's not entirely stupid. She must have felt the sexual tension between us. She was probably doing her best to make sure it never reached explosion point. Which,' he huffed, 'it just has! What time do you expect the others back?'

How could she think of that sort of thing when her mind was spiralling around with happiness, with the deep wonder of all of this? And then she caught his drift and blushed, and he laughed delightedly, touching her scarlet cheeks with the back of his hand as she told him, her words coming out jerkily, 'Petra's spending the night with

Phil's people. He's bringing her back first thing in the morning. And Dad said he'd stop by at Barbara's—for a nightcap. He won't be back before midnight.'

James glanced at his watch. 'That gives us two hours. Not nearly long enough for what I've got in mind.' He was tugging her arms out of her sleeves and his eyes were adoring as they slid over her naked breasts, a catch in his voice as he breathed, 'My God, Zoe, you are beautiful.' He glanced at her, his eyes so soft and deep she could drown in them. 'We marry as soon as it can be arranged. That's not negotiable. Where, is up to you. Agreed?'

'Agreed,' she murmured, busy with his shirt buttons. 'Now will you please stop talking? You're breaking my concentration...'

Coming Next Month

HARLEQUIN PRESENTS®

THE BEST HAS JUST GOTTEN BETTER!

#1845 RELATIVE SINS Anne Mather
Alex mustn't know Sara's secret. But her small son Ben adores him and she has to admit that Alex is ideal father material.... Is the answer to keep it in the family?

#1846 ANGRY DESIRE Charlotte Lamb
(SINS)
Gabriella realized she couldn't marry Stephen and ran out on him on their wedding day. But Stephen wouldn't take "I don't" for an answer....

#1847 RECKLESS CONDUCT Susan Napier
(9 to 5)
Marcus Fox didn't approve of Harriet. She put it down to her new bubbly blond image. Then Marcus reminded her of the events at the last office party....

#1848 THEIR WEDDING DAY Emma Darcy
(This Time, Forever)
Once he was her boss, and her lover.... And now Keir is back in Rowena's life. Can they let go of their past and forge a future together?

#1849 A KISS TO REMEMBER Miranda Lee
(Affairs to Remember)
It was time for Angie to stop comparing every man she met with Lance Sterling and move on. Here she was, twenty-four and a virgin...and suddenly Lance was back in her life!

#1850 FORSAKING ALL OTHERS Susanne McCarthy
When Leo Ratcliffe proposed to Maddie, was he promising the true love of which she'd always dreamed—or merely offering a marriage for his convenience?